MW00454232

MEG ANNE
JESSICA WAYNE

Visions Of Triumph

The Gypsy's Curse, book 3

by Meg Anne & Jessica Wayne

ISBN 13- 978-951738-94-5

Edited by Jessa Russo of Russo Editing

Proofread by Dominique Laura

Cover Design by AV Fantasy Book Cover Art & Design

True love can break the most powerful curse.
-Jodi Picoult

CHAPTER 1

LUCAS

Lungs burning, Lucas pushed himself into a ground-eating sprint as the cottage came into view. While running, he checked the points of entry he could see. The door was still closed, windows unbroken, and although the Druid wouldn't need to break in, it still eased a bit of his panic to find everything looking so normal.

Surely Skye would be inside. He would burst through the door and find her asleep on the couch, and then they would laugh it off over a drink tonight.

Everything's fine. He repeated the mantra, hoping soon he would believe his own words. If only the bone-deep fear taking root in his gut would disappear. It was doing nothing to help reinforce his prayer.

"Skye!" Lucas shouted as he shoved open the door to the cottage, his heart pounding painfully in his chest.

The living room and kitchen were both completely empty and still looked exactly the same as he remembered leaving them. There were no signs of a struggle, so far as he could tell from his spot just inside the doorway. Lucas mentally put another tally in the 'she's safe' column he was slowly building in his mind.

"Skye!" Lizzie repeated, coming in after him, Matthews hot on her heels. His sister's voice bordered on hysteria.

Lucas glanced at them over his shoulder. "I'll grab the bedrooms, you two check the study. And stay together!" he added, already running toward his bedroom.

She has to be here.

He can't have her.

Please don't let him have her.

"Skye!" Lucas called again, the blood thundering in his ears making it impossible for him to hear anything over the sound of his internal terror.

The door to his room was open, so it didn't take more than a passing glance to see that she wasn't inside. Slowing down only long enough to change direction, Lucas sprinted to the room Skye shared with Lizzie when they'd first arrived in Scotland.

It took him less than thirty seconds, but each second without knowing where Skye was felt like a lifetime. When he reached the room, the door was slightly ajar. Lucas forced himself to suck in a breath and slow his racing heart before he nudged the door open with a surprising amount of gentleness, considering the state he was in.

He half-expected—or maybe it was half-hoped—to see Skye curled up in bed, fast asleep with one of her Gran's journals tucked beside her.

But her bed was empty, as was Lizzie's.

Lucas let out a low growl and slammed his fist into the door, sending it crashing into the wall. *Where the fuck is she?* She wouldn't just take off without telling him where she was going. Not with the Druid still out there.

He moved farther into the room, scanning everything like he would a crime scene. A brisk breeze moved through the room, and Lucas' skin erupted in goosebumps. He shivered as he moved to close the window, looking down as he walked past the bed. He paused, focusing on a piece of pale cream paper sticking out from beneath the bed.

Dread coiled in his belly as he knelt and reached for the familiar paper with shaking hands. *It's just a drawing that fell out of her sketchbook.* Lucas flipped the scrap of paper over and breathed a sigh of relief when he recognized Skye's looping script across the page. She must have run into town after all.

The page was stained as if she'd spilled something on it while writing. Lucas didn't look too closely at the small, teardrop-sized splashes. If she left a note, the Druid hadn't gotten to her. She was safe.

His eyes closed and some of the tightness in his chest eased. He'd gotten here in time. Heart returning to a more normal beat, Lucas started to read.

Lucas,

By the time you get this, I'll be gone. I know you won't understand, but please, trust me. I'm doing what's best for both of us. I never imagined meeting you on that balcony would lead to this. I never thought I'd fall in love with you.

I've never cared for a person the way I care for you, and I wish with all of my heart that it was enough, but it isn't.

Not even love is enough to keep me here.

I guess our ancestors knew what they were doing when they vowed to stay away from each other. Gypsies and Druids end up leaving nothing but chaos in their wake when they are together.

It's time to break the cycle.

Do not come after me. There's nothing you could say to make me change my mind. This is the way it has to be.

The way it was always meant to be.

Skye

Numb with shock, Lucas stared at the letter, words blurring and shifting on the page. The piece of paper fluttered to the ground as he struggled to breathe.

She'd left him. This woman he'd *die* for had left him.

A fist tightened around his chest, squeezing his lungs and his heart like a vise. He shook his head as agony consumed him. It didn't make sense.

Lucas' eyes flew open. *What if she'd been forced to leave this note?* Hope flared to life in his chest, and he pulled in a deep breath as he pushed to his feet. He started for the door but paused, turning slowly toward the closet as that knot of dread settled back into his gut. Doors ajar, the closet was empty. Swallowing hard, he turned toward the dresser. He started with the top drawer, pulling it out slowly. Empty. By the time he reached the bottom drawer, he tugged so hard he ripped it right out of the unit. Chest heaving, Lucas threw the empty drawer to the ground.

Empty.

They were *all* empty.

He scanned the room once more, searching for any remaining sign of her as the ugly truth began to sink in.

Skye hadn't been taken. She'd left him.

Willingly.

All because she was too afraid to take a chance on loving him. Could he blame her? Fuck yeah, he could. Skye Giovanni was a lot of things, but he'd never pegged her for a fucking coward.

"Lucas."

He spun around. Bile rising in his throat, he bent to grasp the paper from the floor, crumpling it in his fist before shoving it at Lizzie and Matthews.

"She's gone," he told them.

Lizzie's eyes widened. "Did he—"

"No."

His sister's brows bunched together, and she started to shake her head. "Then I don't understand. Where is she?"

"What's to understand? Skye is a fucking coward. She bailed on us." Lucas pushed past them, saying all he'd intended to say on the matter.

He'd loved her, body and soul. She'd told him she loved him, too, and Lucas had believed her. Turns out he'd been nothing but a way to pass the fucking time. Regardless of what her words read, when you loved someone, you stood beside them. No matter what.

She hadn't loved him; she'd made a fool of him.

Lucas pulled a bottle of scotch from the cabinet and drank deeply, not taking the time to fill a glass with the amber liquid that reminded him of Skye's eyes. The burn in his throat was nothing compared to the ache in his chest, so he ignored it, opting instead for the numbness the alcohol would bring. At this point, he'd kill for just a bit of relief from the pain of her leaving.

Lizzie snatched the bottle from his hand, sending droplets flying as she slammed it down on the counter. "Stop drinking like you're some kind of fucking fish."

He glared at her, and to her credit, she didn't flinch. "I can do whatever the hell I want," Lucas growled.

"Do you seriously not see what this is?" She shook the tiny scrap of paper in his face as Matthews came to stand beside her.

"It's a fucking 'Dear John'," Lucas said simply. "She didn't even have the decency to tell me to my face. She waited until we were gone so she could sneak out of here like the coward she is."

"I know we haven't known Skye long, but we all know she is *not* a coward," Lizzie argued.

Lucas pointed aggressively at the piece of paper in her hand. "That note proves otherwise."

"Did it ever even cross your mind the Druid made her leave that for you to find? That this is all some elaborate game of his and that maybe he threatened her?" Lizzie shoved the paper in his face. "These are tear stains, Lucas. Which means she hadn't wanted to leave it."

Lucas shook his head. "No fucking way. Do you really think that bastard would want me to think she left? He would have bragged about taking her, would have rubbed it in my face that he had her. Shame will make you cry, too, and if I was leaving my friends and the person I claimed to love behind to deal with a psychopath on their own, I'd sure as hell be ashamed."

Lizzie stared at him, eyes wide with disbelief. She turned to his partner for help. "James, talk some sense into him."

Matthews put his hands up. "Sorry, Lizzie, the Druid's an arrogant prick. It's not far-fetched to think he would taunt Lucas if he could. It doesn't take a profiler to figure that out."

Her mouth gaped as she looked between the two of them. She shook her head, scoffing. "You two are fucking unbelievable." She banged her fist down onto the counter, sending the scotch teetering off the side and shattering on the ground.

The liquid pooled on the floor, and Lucas scowled at his sister. "That's a fucking waste, Elizabeth."

She winced. He never used her full name, and it's use now had the effect he'd hoped for.

"You and your arrogant know-it-all attitude are a waste. I sure as hell hope I never get taken. I'd hate to think the two of you would give up on me so easily. You call her a coward?" Lizzie slammed the note down on the counter. "You two are the fucking cowards for not wanting to face something just because your macho feelings were hurt."

Lucas glared at her, his upper lip curled in a snarl. "You think accepting that she willingly left me is easy?"

His voice was low, but his sister's eyes were wide, and she took a tentative step back.

Power bloomed inside him, answering the rage building in his chest.

"I fucking love her; do you understand that?" he roared. "Believing the Druid took her would be the easy way out, because it would mean I didn't have to accept that she didn't love me, too!"

The kitchen window shattered, and Lizzie whimpered.

Matthews pulled Lizzie behind him and stood tall. "You need to chill the fuck out, Lucas."

"Why? Am I not allowed to be pissed off?"

"Sure, be pissed. Hell, go punch a fucking hole in the wall, but don't you dare take it out on the one person who believes in you more than anyone else."

Lucas swallowed hard and looked behind Matthews' shoulder at his sister. She was bone-white, her cheeks losing their flush from her mad dash to the cottage. Pupils dilated with fear, they'd all but erased the bright blue of her irises. She regarded him like a cornered animal and he was the predator. Was that what he was becoming?

He straightened and reached into the cabinet for another bottle. "Leave me alone."

"Not a damn problem." Matthews took Lizzie's hand and led her out of the room.

Lucas took a deep drink from the bottle.

Giving Skye the benefit of the doubt was foolish. She'd left, and now they were all going to have to figure out how the fuck to move on without her.

Even if that meant Lucas ended up drinking himself to death.

CHAPTER 2

SKYE

Skye's eyes fluttered open, and she pressed the heels of her hands against them. Pain radiated through the back of her neck and up into her forehead. Her right side ached as if she'd been repeatedly kicked by someone much larger than herself.

What happened to me?

She rubbed at her eyes, praying for relief that didn't come. Giving up, Skye removed her hands and squinted, trying to focus on her surroundings.

Where am I?

The walls and ceiling of whatever building she was in were made of brick, as was the hard floor she was lying on. A single metal folding chair was the only furniture in the room. Looking up she counted six small windows, which were caked with dirt and grime. This was obviously not a place people frequented on any kind of regular basis.

Skye swallowed hard. So, it hadn't been a nightmare. The Druid really did kidnap her.

What the hell am I going to do? Am I even in Scotland anymore?

Weak light pouring in through one of the dusty windows pulled her attention. Skye pushed to her feet. Maybe she could determine where she was by looking outside. Her stomach twisted as a loud scraping sound filled the heavy silence. Dread pooled in her belly at the sight of the heavy chain latched around her ankle. *The fucker chained me to the wall.*

She wasn't going anywhere.

Bright blue eyes flashed through her mind, and her heart gave a painful lurch. *Lucas.* Skye slowly fell back to her knees, curling herself into a tight ball. How long would it be before he discovered she was gone? What would he do? Would he come after her? *Of course not, you jackass, you told him not to.* Skye's heart broke all over again at the reminder of the note she'd left him.

She hadn't meant a word of it, other than that she was very much in love with him. But she'd needed to make it believable so he wouldn't follow her. A fact that was really going to bite her in the ass now that he was the only person who could save her.

If hurting the man she loved wasn't damning enough, by leaving that note, she'd essentially signed their collective death warrants. Skye wasn't an idiot; she knew the Druid wouldn't leave the others alone now that he had her. Her vision would still come to pass.

They always did.

She should have known better than to try and change fate.

"You're a fucking idiot, Giovanni," Skye muttered as

tears burned in the corners of her eyes. A lump in her throat made it damn near impossible to breathe.

"Good, you're awake."

Skye's head shot up. *Speak of the devil…*

She twisted as the Druid walked into the room from a doorway set in the farthest wall. He wore his cloak, but the hood was pulled back, giving her a full view of his scarred face and those eerie black eyes. He grinned, and her fists clenched so hard her nails bit into the tender skin of her palm.

"You fucking bastard," she growled through clenched teeth.

He clicked his tongue. "Ah-ah-ah. That's not a very ladylike attitude, Seer."

"I never claimed to be a lady, asshole. And who the hell do you think you are, trying to teach me manners? You're the furthest thing from a gentleman."

The Druid laughed, the joyful outburst more terrifying for its sincerity. It couldn't be a good sign that he was so happy.

"You aren't wrong there," he murmured as he made his way across the brick floor, taking a seat in a folding chair just out of reach of her tether. "Thanks for making it so easy for me, by the way. A goodbye note? I hadn't even thought of that."

"Lucas is going to come for me, and when he does, he's going to tear you apart."

"I very much doubt that. Your note will have broken his pathetic heart. He won't be doing anything but drowning in liquor, which will admittedly make my job even easier."

Even though the Druid's words closely echoed her earlier thoughts, Skye didn't hesitate as she spat, "You're wrong. He's stronger than you are."

"You keep telling yourself that, Seer, if it makes you feel better. Besides, he won't be finding you until I want him to." Leaning forward in his chair, he dropped his voice to a conspiratorial whisper. "And right now, I don't want him to."

Her heart raced, but she didn't give him the satisfaction of a response.

When Skye only continued to stare at him from her place on the floor, he got to his feet. She scooted back, pressing herself into the wall as much as she could, but he kept coming, kneeling directly in front of her.

"Don't you fucking touch me," she warned, slapping at his hand when he gripped the bottom of her shirt.

He smiled at her, a cold, terrifying grin. The hand not touching her began to glow, and Skye's arms flew away from his and to the side of her body. She was completely frozen, his power turning her into a statue, leaving her absolutely unable to do anything to stop him. He ripped her shirt up to just below her breasts and gestured to her right side.

Skye looked down and fought a wave of nausea. The bastard had carved a rune into her side, a brand that would permanently mar her skin. And she hadn't even felt it. She wasn't sure which was worse, that he'd marked her, or that she had been completely unaware of the liberties he'd taken with her body.

What else did the bastard do while I was out cold?

"This is my own personal blend of magic." He stroked

the lines of the symbol lovingly, as a normal person might do with a drawing their child made for them.

She winced, inwardly recoiling from his caress even as she was helpless to actually pull away from him physically. Each brush of his fingers against her skin sent sharp bolts of pain through the rest of her body.

"It blocks you from any and all tracking, except mine." He winked and stepped back, releasing her from his magical hold.

Skye spat at him. The resulting crack across her face sent her head slamming back into the brick, causing stars to explode in her vision.

"I own you, Seer. There's not a damn thing you can do about it. The sooner you realize that, the sooner we'll start getting along."

"You. Do. Not. Fucking. Own. Me!" Skye screamed, furious tears streaming down her cheeks.

The Druid reached back down and grabbed her by the throat. She clawed at his hands as he lifted her off the ground and held her right at eye level.

"I could crush you right now, extinguish your pathetic life force along with your smartass attitude." He tightened his grasp. "Should I? Should I just end you now? Or should I wait until my grandson is here to watch you die?"

Skye forced herself to return his stare, not wanting to show any weakness by looking away, despite the fact her vision was fading.

The Druid pressed his nose against hers. "Tell me, Seer. What do you See? My victory?"

"I. See. Your. Death. You. Miserable. Bastard," she choked out.

He pulled her away from the wall just long enough to slam her back against it, the clank of her chain a jarring punctuation. He pressed his lips to the side of her face, trailing them up to her ear, where he paused to whisper, "Soon, you'll learn not to taunt me, Seer."

Revulsion crawled across her body like an army of spiders. *Hide the fear, Giovanni. Don't let him know he's getting to you.*

"You obviously don't know me at all," she retorted with as much disdain as she could muster.

He laughed and dropped her to the ground. Skye gasped for air, pushing back to her feet. If he came close like that again, she was going to kick him right in his fucking balls.

The Druid took his seat again and stared at her like she was a bug under a magnifying glass. Was taunting him until he killed her really such a great idea? Probably not. But if it meant dying now instead of in that field in front of Lucas, she'd gladly sacrifice her life to save him from becoming the monster she'd Seen.

Lucas was more important.

"I'm curious about something, Seer. My grandson seems to have quite an attachment to you. So, why would you leave?"

"None of your fucking business."

"Did you see him lose? Did you run to save yourself?"

Skye pinned him with her angriest stare.

"That's it, isn't it?" The Druid laughed. "Didn't think you'd give up so easily; you seemed to have a bit more fight in you than that. Not that I'm complaining, mind you. Just intrigued."

"I didn't give up," she growled.

"You ran to save your skin, leaving those you'd pledged loyalty to behind. Does that sound like fighting to you? What else would you call that, if not giving up?"

Skye ignored him and turned to look at the window.

"Why do you fight it?"

Her eyes darted back to him. His black gaze was still narrowed on her face as if he studied her beneath a microscope. "Fight what, exactly?" she asked sweetly.

"Me."

The absurdity of the question made her want to laugh. "Let's see, should I start with reason number one? Or two-thousand? Because I have lots of fucking reasons."

"You know you will lose."

"I might, but Lucas won't."

The Druid shook his head. "Seer, you have truly placed your faith in the wrong member of my line. I will kill him, his sister, that pathetic detective that thinks he can protect her, and then finally you."

"Why wait? You have me now. Just kill me and get it over with."

He smiled at her, and the sight of it sent shivers of fear down her spine.

"And let my grandson miss it? I want him front and center when his Gypsy whore dies by my hand." The Druid stood. "This has been an even more entertaining conversation than I had hoped. Now, if you'll excuse me, I have some preparations to make. I want to be sure to have everything ready when it's time to let my grandson come find you."

"No matter what you do, he will kill you! I've Seen it!"

Pausing, the Druid turned back to face her. "Have you? Because based on that letter you left him, I'd guess you've Seen just the opposite."

Angry tears pooled in her eyes.

"Rest well, Seer. Not that it matters… you'll be dead soon." With a final sinister smile, the Druid left.

The door slammed behind him, and Skye stared at it a moment before a rush of tears spilled down her cheeks. Her shoulders shook with the force of her weeping. A dam had burst within her, letting a tidal wave of emotion break free.

Anger at herself.

Fear for those she loved.

Terror at Seeing a soulless Lucas destroy everyone and everything he'd ever cared about.

What have I done?

CHAPTER 3

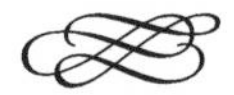

LIZZIE

Lucas was slumped down in one of the plaid armchairs, his legs sprawled out in front of him. He tilted the mostly empty bottle of scotch against his lips and stared mutinously off into the corner of the living room.

Lizzie scowled and shook her head. *What the hell is wrong with him?* This wasn't her brother. He'd been sitting like that for the past four hours. Lizzie couldn't believe he'd just given up, it was so unlike him. She knew his heart was hurting, but that was no excuse to admit defeat. Especially not when the woman he loved was out there, needing him to come to her rescue. He was a fucking detective, for God's sake. This shit was what he lived for.

Lizzie didn't believe for a minute that Skye left of her own free will. Maybe Skye had thought she was doing the right thing, but she loved Lucas too much to stay away forever. She would have changed her mind and come back before she'd gotten far.

Why am I the only one that can see it?

"Fucking men," she muttered darkly, moving through the house and back toward the hall.

"Where are you going?" James asked, peeking his head out from their room.

Lizzie glared at him. She'd refused to talk to him ever since he took her brother's side in his bullshit argument.

James frowned and moved to stand in the doorway. Lizzie forced herself to ignore the way his shirt pulled across his pecs. He didn't deserve her lusting after him.

"Seriously, Liz? How old are we?"

She raised a brow and folded her arms over her chest.

He took a step toward her, and Lizzie shuffled back. She'd cave if he touched her, and she wasn't ready to let him off the hook. If they were going to be together, he needed to learn that she wasn't just his partner's pea-brained little sister. He needed to weigh her ideas just as seriously as he did her brother's.

"Lizzie." Her name came out half-groan, half-whine, and she would have laughed if she still wasn't so angry.

How could both men forget what Skye had done for them? Did no one but her care that Skye was out there all alone? That she was the only reason they were still alive? Had Skye not gone out on a limb and warned Lucas, the Druid would have gotten her that first night in her diner. They owed her their lives.

"Come on, Liz. Don't shut me out like this. I'm sorry."

"For what?"

James' brows knit together. "That I hurt your feelings."

Lizzie's anger continued to simmer. Lucas wasn't the only MacConnell who could nurse a grudge. She canted her head to the side. "What did you do to hurt my feelings, James?"

"I took your brother's side…" he trailed off, looking confused.

Lizzie shoved her finger into his chest. "No, James. I'm not upset that you took my brother's side. I'm pissed that you wouldn't even consider what I was saying for a fucking minute before you completely dismissed me!"

James' brows flew up, but she was just getting started.

"You call yourself a detective? Look at the fucking evidence in front of you."

Now it was his turn to glower. "I did look at the evidence, Liz. She left him a damned note."

"Covered in tear stains! She was fucking sobbing while she wrote that, James. There's no way in hell she wanted to leave him. You saw the two of them together—she is head over heels in love with him. You don't just walk away from that."

James sucked on his cheek, his hazel eyes going thoughtful. After a moment, his shoulders dropped, and he took a deep breath. "She still packed a bag and left the note for Lucas to find. Maybe she was torn up about leaving, but it doesn't change the fact that she took off."

Lizzie opened her mouth to protest, but James held up a hand.

"Let me finish. There wasn't a sign of struggle, Liz. No forced entry, nothing out of place." James' voice was soft and apologetic. "I'm sorry, babe. But given the *facts*, I just don't see how you can arrive at any other conclusion."

"Then you obviously know sweet fuck all when it

comes to a woman in love," she sneered, turning away from him.

"What the hell is that supposed to mean?" he called after her.

"You want evidence, Detective? I'll find your damned evidence," she muttered, stalking back into the room where Lucas found Skye's letter.

There must be something they'd overlooked, and Lizzie was going to find it and shove it down their damn throats.

Two hours later, Lizzie had nothing to show for her search except a monster of a mess. She'd left no stone unturned, literally. The beds had been shoved out of their spaces, the blankets tossed to the side. The drawers were already on the floor from Lucas' search, and what had been left inside the closet was scattered along the top of the now naked mattresses.

Someone knocked softly on the door, and she looked up from the books in her lap, but the door opened before she could tell whichever annoying male was on the other side to fuck off.

James glanced around the room, his face carefully neutral. "You, uh, redecorating?"

She glared at him. "Yup. Felt like a great time for it."

He studied her carefully. "Find anything?"

Lizzie deflated. "Not yet."

"Why don't you leave this mess for a while and come make some dinner."

Her head snapped back up. “Excuse me?”

James winced at her screech. “Uh, dinner?” He gestured toward the kitchen.

“Let me get this straight, James Amadeus Matthews—”

He grimaced.

“—because I must not have heard you correctly. You want me to stop searching for a clue about what might have happened to my best friend because you want me to *cook you dinner*?”

“You promised never to use my middle name.”

Lizzie stood slowly, books and a few loose pieces of paper falling to the floor. “As if I give a flying fuck about your unfortunate middle name right now.”

“I just thought…”

She put her hands on her hips. “What did you just think, James? I’m so interested in hearing this explanation.”

His cheeks were tinged a bright red. “Cooking always seems to calm you down.”

Lizzie grit her teeth, her voice going dangerously soft. “Do I look like I need to calm down to you?”

“Yes?” James replied, barely ducking in time when Lizzie launched a book at his head.

“Get out!” she screeched.

“Lizzie…”

“I swear to God, James Matthews, if you come back in here right now, I am going to throat punch you.”

There was a scuffle outside the door, as if he was resisting the urge to try again. “I was just trying to help,” he finally mumbled, before walking away.

Lizzie listened to his fading footsteps and sighed. What was it about men that had them saying the exact wrong thing when they only meant to be helpful? It was like some cosmic practical joke. They were just hardwired for it.

She sighed. Cooking would definitely help her clear her head, but she'd be damned if those two asshats got a free meal out of her. They could fend for themselves.

Glancing around the room, Lizzie groaned. If she didn't start putting things away, she would have to be excavated out of here.

"Might as well start with the bookcase," she muttered, climbing over piles of clothes and books to grab the one she'd hurled at James.

Straightening, a dark smear on the doorframe caught her eye. *Has that always been here?*

She checked the book in her hand, wondering if some of the paint had transferred when it hit the wood. The book was bright green. That was a definite no.

Squinting, she leaned closer to the wood, her finger hovering over the almost black smear. What if this was evidence? Should she touch it?

"What is that?" she asked, her heart pounding.

Leaning even closer, Lizzie made out a few strands of what appeared to be dark hair stuck to the smear. She sucked in a breath, suddenly light-headed.

"James," she called, her voice sounding far away even to her own ears. When she didn't immediately hear foot-steps, she screamed, "James!"

"Lizzie, what's wrong?" He quickly appeared in the doorway.

With a shaking finger, she pointed to the hair and what

she was starting to believe must be blood on the doorframe.

"I think I found something."

James followed the line of her finger and returned his eyes to hers. "What is it?"

"I'm pretty sure that's a chunk of Skye's hair."

Surprise flared in James' eyes, and he leaned closer to the door.

"Still think she left on her own?" Lizzie asked.

He straightened and turned to face her. "I don't know what to think."

"Should we tell Lucas?"

James shook his head. "He's in no state to process anything right now. Let him sleep it off. In the meantime, you and I need to see if there's anything else to indicate that Skye might have been hurt."

Lizzie nodded, her eyes meeting James' worried ones.

He wrapped his arms around her and pulled her into a tight hug. "I'm sorry I didn't believe you. You did good, Liz. I'm sorry for being such an ass."

She should have felt vindicated, hearing James admit that he'd been wrong, but all she felt was hollow and scared. Who wanted to be right about their friend being kidnapped?

Even worse, Skye was out there somewhere, alone and probably terrified, and they didn't have a fucking clue where to start looking for her.

CHAPTER 4

LUCAS

"So, tell me, Detective..." Skye lifted her head off of his chest and looked up at him with amber eyes that seemed to see directly into his soul. "What's something you've always wanted to do?"

"You mean besides this?" Lucas ran his hands up her bare back and cupped her face before pressing his lips to hers.

The feel of her against him, skin to skin, was more than he ever believed he'd find. Skye laughed, and he soaked up the melody as if it were the first and last time he'd ever hear it.

"Yes, besides this."

Moonlight bathed her in an ethereal glow, making her bronze skin appear like it was illuminated from within.

"Hmmm. I can't really focus on anything else at the moment." He kissed her deeply, and she molded her body against his, a perfect fit.

Skye pulled away and sat up, straddling him while the blankets pooled at her waist. Lucas put his arm behind his head and stared up at her. Dark, nearly midnight hair fell in loose waves to the middle of her back, and he reached up with his other arm to twirl it in his fingers. The silky strands slipped through them as she leaned down to kiss him again.

Lucas pulled her hard against his body, savoring the taste and feel of her. To him, there would never be anyone as amazing as her, no one who completed him so perfectly. She was it, his always and forever.

She sat back and smiled softly at him. "You make me feel whole, Detective. Thank you for that."

He started to respond when a sharp, stabbing pain surged through his chest as if someone had driven a knife down into his heart. Lucas clutched at his chest and looked up at Skye. The light had faded, and tears fell from her eyes, streaming down her pale cheeks. She looked both heartbroken and terrified.

"I love you, Lucas," she whispered.

His breaths came in sharp bursts, the pain in his chest making it nearly impossible to breathe. "What the hell is happening?"

"I love you, Lucas," she repeated. "I will always love you, please don't forget that." She began to fade away.

"Skye!" He reached for her, but the pain sent him falling back onto the mattress.

Still clutching his chest where his heart ached like it had been torn out of his body, Lucas started to sit up. A dark shadow in the corner of the room caught his eye as it peeled itself away from the wall, moving into a pool of moonlight pouring in from the open window. Lucas growled as the shadow solidified.

The Druid stood wrapped in his dark cloak, smiling down at him, the scar on the bastard's face making him appear more monster than man. Anger pulsed through Lucas as he stared into the obsidian eyes that had haunted him since that night in the diner.

"What are you doing here?" Lucas attempted to get to his feet, but his shaking legs couldn't support his weight, and he sat down hard on the bed.

The Druid said nothing, just continued to stare at him with that same sinister smile playing about his lips. Finally, he disappeared just as Skye had, leaving Lucas alone, terrified, and in unbelievable agony.

LIGHT POURED IN THROUGH THE WINDOWS, SETTING Lucas' head on fire. He groaned and rolled over. *Did I get hit by a fucking truck?* Still not entirely clear of the blinding light, Lucas tried to turn away further and started to fall.

"Shit!" He landed on the floor with an *oomph* and rolled onto his back, eyes closed as tightly as he could manage. *So, I'm in the living room*. No fucking wonder his body was stiff; he'd passed out on the ancient couch.

"Hope that hurt."

"Not now, Lizzie." He groaned again and rubbed his eyes with the backs of his hands. *Skye was gone*. A fresh wave of suffocating pain surged through him, and Lucas fought against the burn of tears.

Never in his life had anyone ever had such a hold on him. After a handful of weeks, she'd managed to barrel into his life and turn him inside out. Apparently, one of Skye Giovanni's mystical powers was to turn him into a complete fucking wreck.

The scent of freshly brewed coffee filled his nose, but it didn't hold the same alluring power it had before. All it meant now was the start of another day without her.

"Hey, man, want some coffee?"

Lucas peered out through his fingers.

Matthews stood above him, cup in hand.

"Scotch," he grunted.

"I think you've had enough alcohol to last you a good while. You're going to kill yourself if you keep it up."

"Sounds like a plan to me."

"I think it's time you stop acting so fucking pathetic."

Lucas pushed to his feet, ignoring the jackhammer in his temples. "Are you fucking kidding me?"

He got nose to nose with his partner, the man who'd been his best friend for over a decade. Lucas was proud of himself for only swaying once.

"You heard what I said. If you'd stop wallowing in self-pity for two seconds, we might be able to have a real conversation about the possibility that Skye didn't leave willingly."

Lucas rolled his eyes and stepped back. "What the fuck is it with you two and taking her side? She fucking left me!" he roared. "You two are supposed to be on *my team*. Or have you forgotten that?"

"We're not against you, Lucas. If you'd put on your big boy panties for one damn minute, you'd see that," Lizzie said from the kitchen.

"Yeah, I'm fucking sure about that." Not interested in

hearing the two traitors take her side one second longer, Lucas headed for the glass doors that led to the back patio.

"Where the hell are you going?" Matthews asked, on his heels.

"None of your fucking business." He slammed the door behind him, hoping it clipped his partner in the face, and stalked toward the hill behind the cottage. Barefoot and in a T-shirt, cold air nipped at him, but Lucas couldn't care less about it. Hell, maybe he'd freeze to death out here; then everything would be over.

No more pain.

No more fucking Druid to deal with.

At the top of the small hill, Lucas took a seat and stared down at the cabin, scowling. *Why the hell didn't they get it?* If Matthews took off on Lizzie, Lucas would do whatever he could to make her feel better. Shit, if she ditched his partner with some stupid fucking note, he'd confront her and figure out just what the hell she'd been thinking.

So, why wouldn't they do the same for him?

Why did it have to be all about Skye and what *she'd* gone through?

Seething, he pushed to his feet. Hungover or not, Lucas needed to run until his lungs gave out. Stretching his arms, he turned, and a blur of color on the ground near the side of the house caught his attention.

Curious, Lucas made his way back down the hill and walked to the side of the house where Lizzie and Skye's bedroom window was. He bent, unsure what to make of his find as he lifted one of Skye's scarves from the ground. The soft material slipped like silk over his fingertips, and he held it up to his nose to breathe in her scent.

Except, it wasn't just Skye he could smell on the fabric. Lucas wasn't sure how he'd even picked up the other scent, perhaps his magic had heightened his senses, but something wasn't right with it. It smelled…*wrong*.

Lucas carried the scarf into the house, and both his sister and partner turned to watch him, faces guarded, as he made his way into the kitchen. Matthews stood beside Lizzie, arms folded, ready for a fight.

Lucas thrust the scarf at him. "Smell it."

"Excuse me?"

"Smell it."

"Why?"

"Because I want to know what you pick up."

Matthews held the scarf up to his nose and inhaled. "It smells like grass." He handed it to Lizzie, who stared down at it, tears in her eyes.

"You ready to listen now?" she asked Lucas.

"For the record, I still think she left willingly," he told her. "But I'm willing to listen to why you think she didn't."

"'Bout fucking time, dickhead. Let's go."

Lucas and Matthews followed Lizzie into the room she'd shared with Skye. She stopped just inside the door and pointed to the doorframe.

"What am I looking at?"

"You'll see it," Lizzie insisted.

Lucas refocused on the door jam, his eyes scanning the wood, not seeing anything but chipped paint. He was just about to give up when he finally saw it. A faint dark stain against the wood grain. Leaning closer, he detected strands of dark hair smeared in the dried blood.

"We think it might be Skye's," Matthews told him.

Lucas nodded absently, heart at war with what his gut was telling him. He'd recognize her hair anywhere; the dark midnight strands were forever burned into his memory. The corresponding flare of hope the discovery caused was almost more painful than the grief he'd been wallowing in.

There was nothing Lucas wanted to believe more than that Skye hadn't left him. But facts were facts. She'd written that note, which meant that at some point she'd had every intention of walking out on him. Could he ever forgive her for that?

Taking a deep breath, he forced himself to focus only on the evidence before him and not on the painful thumping of his battered heart.

The note didn't fit with being kidnapped, which meant that either Skye planned to leave him and changed her mind, or she'd been on her way out when the Druid grabbed her.

Either way, Skye hadn't left by herself. She'd been taken, and Lucas was going to get her the fuck back, even if it meant risking her leaving him all over again.

CHAPTER 5

SKYE

Skye opened her eyes slowly, not ready to let go of the dream image of Lucas smiling up at her. Salty tears rolled down her cheeks, and her heart lurched in her chest. For one glorious moment, she'd forgotten. She'd been back in bed, curled up with Lucas, and he'd kissed her with so much love that she'd been filled with it.

If he ever sets his eyes on you again, the last thing you're going to see is love.

A soft whimper escaped as Skye rolled to her side and curled into a ball.

"Sweet dreams?"

Skye pushed herself into a sitting position, barely suppressing a moan as searing heat flared in her side. The Druid had been watching her sleep. Her lip curled up in disgust.

He studied her from the chair, his head tilted, and his black eyes narrowed. "You were smiling and making the sweetest little sounds."

Skye's stomach rolled. Him watching her when she

was in such a vulnerable state was just another violation in a seemingly endless list. He was the worst kind of voyeur, stealing personal moments he was not entitled to. She *hated* that he knew what kinds of sounds she made while she was sleeping. It grossed her out almost as much as finding out he'd touched her while she'd been unconscious.

Narrowing her eyes, she glared at him.

"So fierce, little Seer." He chuckled and settled back in his chair. "If you aren't going to be good company, then I might as well return to my reading."

Skye recognized the leather-bound book he was holding, and she was up and moving toward him without conscious thought. It wasn't until the chain went taut and threw her off balance, that Skye remembered she was stuck.

She hit the brick floor with a slap of skin and rattle of chains, her elbows and chin taking the brunt of the impact. Tiny stars exploded behind her eyes, and her mouth filled with blood. Eyes tearing, Skye spat a mouthful of blood on the ground.

"My, my, what a reaction. Could it be there's something in here you don't want me to find?"

"Those are my grandmother's journals." The quaver in her voice undermined any trace of her righteous fury.

Unmoving, he stared at her. "What's your point?"

"You have no right to read them, you bastard."

The Druid laughed. "Doesn't seem like there's much you can do to stop me."

Ignoring the stinging in her palms and knees, Skye pushed off the ground and back to her feet.

"Pity," he murmured. "I am growing to enjoy the sight of you on your knees before me."

Lifting her chin, she stared down the length of her nose at him, even though they were practically the same height. Trying to infuse her voice with as much disdain as possible, she growled, "Fuck off."

His smile faded, and his eyes grew darker as if any residual trace of humanity had fled. There was nothing human about the man as he stood and began to slowly stalk forward.

Skye's instincts screamed at her to run, but she locked her muscles, refusing to budge even an inch. For all her bravado, she was helpless against the impossibly fast backhand that sent her plummeting back to the ground. This time, she landed hip first and bounced once before rolling onto her back with a pitiful moan.

The Druid squatted down, using a single finger to tilt her chin until her eyes met his.

"When will you realize that I own you, little girl? I will not tolerate your disrespect." His soulless eyes deliberately roamed over her body, until returning to hers. "No matter your other, considerable, charms."

She was shaking with rage, the words she wanted to hurl back at him lodged in her throat. Skye was a lot of things, but she was not stupid. Her odds of getting through this alive were slim at best. Not only did he have her chained up, he had her grandmother's journals, and his fucking brand made it impossible for Lucas to find her. She was totally and completely screwed. There was no handsome prince coming to save her. She was one damsel that was going to have to figure out how to save herself.

Or at least prolong what was left of her life long enough to buy Lucas time.

That meant she needed to learn how to play the Druid's game. Even though every fiber of her being wanted to claw his perverted eyes out.

Skye forced herself to swallow back her anger. Let him think that he'd gotten to her. "S-sorry," she stuttered, no longer trying to stop her limbs from trembling.

He stroked the length of her hair, and Skye hoped her shudder of revulsion only appeared to be more quaking limbs.

"There's my good girl. Now, tell me, what does *amria* mean?"

Jaw clenched, Skye bit down on her lip and shook her head, staring up at the Druid with wide eyes. "I-I don't know."

The Druid tsked. "Ah, but I think you do. Tell me," he demanded, his voice barely more than a snarl.

Skye shook her head. "I don't know."

His eyes narrowed, and he let out a long sigh. "Ah, Skye. Here I was thinking you were ready to be a good girl. I guess I need to teach you a few more lessons."

He shifted, grabbing her hand and stroking his fingers along the back of it. "It's alright," he murmured. "Every good dog needs to be broken."

Horror replaced disgust as his intentions became clear. "No!"

There was a loud crack as the Druid snapped Skye's finger, leaving it jutting out at an awkward ninety-degree angle. She screamed until her voice went hoarse.

"Now, let's try that again." His voice was a silky

croon. He could have been talking to a child or even a lover. “What does *amria* mean, Skye?”

“I don’t”—she panted, pain making it difficult to breathe—“know.”

The Druid leaned forward, his eyes all that she could make out as her vision swam. “Liar,” he breathed, grasping her forearm with both his hands.

A lone tear rolled down her cheek. “Please,” she begged.

This time, it wasn’t a finger he broke, and Skye wasn’t conscious long enough to scream.

CHAPTER 6

LUCAS

"We have to focus, lad," Giles insisted.

Lucas closed his eyes. *Focus, he says... because that's such an easy fucking task with people watching me*. "I'm trying," he gritted out, actively trying not to glare at the older man.

Exasperated, Giles shook his head. "We're never going to find her this way." Getting up from his seat on the couch, he stormed into the kitchen.

"Well, he's in a mood," Lizzie commented dryly from an armchair in the corner.

"He's not the only one," Lucas muttered, still sitting cross-legged on the floor.

He felt like a fucking idiot. Never having put much stock in forced meditation or any of that shit, the idea that it might help him access his magic long enough to track Skye nearly had him laughing. He hadn't had to act like a hippie when he'd used magic before, why was this any different?

"You know," Lizzie started, "meditation has been proven to help people."

"Yeah, okay." Lucas got to his feet and headed into the now empty kitchen. *Old man's probably in the study looking for a* Druidry for Dummies *book to share with me.*

Two days had passed since he'd found Skye's scarf. Two days of knowing she wasn't safe, but rather in the clutches of a monster who wanted them all dead. Lucas' hand clenched into a fist, and he closed his eyes against the onslaught of emotion.

What if she is already dead?

"Lucas," Lizzie said softly.

He opened his eyes and looked at his sister, who watched him with no small amount of concern. "What?"

"You have to calm down."

At his incredulous look, she pointed to his left hand, which rested on the countertop. After lifting it, Lucas saw the impression of a handprint he'd unknowingly burned into the smooth surface.

"Sorry," he muttered, although he wasn't really.

The only thing he was sorry for was leaving Skye alone. He hadn't wanted to split up in the first place. He should have trusted his instincts and forced her to go with them into town. Lucas snorted. Like anyone could force Skye to do anything. Even so, if he'd tried harder then, she wouldn't be fucking gone now. The phrase 'hindsight is twenty-twenty' had never pissed him off more than it did now.

"You have to stop beating yourself up."

"Can you get the fuck out of my head, Lizzie?"

She shrugged. "You're my brother, I can't help it."

Lizzie wrapped her arms around him, and Lucas hesitated for a moment before returning the embrace.

"We'll find her."

"But in what shape? You've seen what a psycho he is, Lizzie. What if he—" Lucas' words broke off before he could give voice to his worst fear.

"You have to have faith in us, in her. Skye's tough, we'll find her."

"What's up?" Matthews asked as he stepped into the kitchen with a half-eaten apple in his hand.

"Giles stormed out on us," Lucas informed him.

"He'll be back. I heard him cussing on the back porch a second ago. What'd you do to piss him off?"

"He's pretty shaken up about Skye's kidnapping," Lizzie answered.

Matthews nodded in understanding. "We have anything yet?"

Lucas shook his head. "I'm not sure if it's even possible to track someone magically, but if so, I can't sense her."

"We'll find her, man. I'm going to hit the books in the study, see if we can find some way to pull the bastard out of whatever hole he's in."

The back door slammed, and Giles stomped into the kitchen, his wrinkled face red. "Ye ready to try again?"

"This isn't working." Lucas folded his arms. "There has to be something else, some other way of figuring out where he has her. Maybe back in Chicago?"

"Why would he leave when we're here? It doesn't make sense." Lizzie bit down on her bottom lip in contemplation. "He needs us—or at least you—to finish his ritual, so doesn't it make sense he'd be keeping her close by?"

Lucas considered. "Possibly. Maybe we head to town, do some canvassing and see if we can find anything to lead us back to him?"

"Seems like a good plan," Matthews agreed. "But you need some sleep. You can't live on coffee alone, and by my guess, you haven't slept since you almost drank yourself into a coma two days ago."

"I'm fine."

"You aren't going to be any good to her if you can't stand on your own feet," Matthews argued.

"Ye need to rest so ye can access yer magic when necessary," Giles agreed.

"Thought you were all about tracking her magically?" Lucas shot at the old man.

"Ye obviously aren't up for it."

The words cut deep, and Lucas scowled.

Ignoring him, Giles continued, "We need to get our Seer back, so if that means we do it yer way, then that's fine by me. I'll work on translatin' the rest of the book."

He turned and left the kitchen, and Lucas watched him take a seat on the couch.

"Go get some sleep." Lizzie kissed his cheek, and she and Matthews headed down the hall toward the study.

Resigned, Lucas made his way to his bedroom. It seemed so empty without Skye, as if she were the color in his world, and without her, things had gone dark.

Why the hell should he be sleeping when she was quite possibly fighting for her life right now? In what world was that acceptable?

He plopped back on the mattress, his head hitting a pillow that still smelled like her, and closed his eyes.

"Skye," he whispered, his voice breaking. "Where the hell are you?"

LUCAS OPENED HIS EYES AND ROLLED OVER IN THE DARK. His hand brushed bare skin, and he shot out of bed, crossing the room to hit the light switch.

"Skye?" he asked, hope and disbelief thickening his voice as his eyes adjusted.

"Lucas?"

Her amber eyes had lost some of their fire and were surrounded by dark circles. He walked back over to their bed slowly and brushed a strand of dark hair from her face.

"You okay?"

"I am now," she whispered, her voice strained. "I miss you."

"But I'm right here."

"Kiss me." She sat up.

She was fully dressed, unlike in his last dream. Her shirt was torn, and it was the same outfit she'd been wearing when he'd last seen her at the cottage.

Lucas knelt beside her on the bed and cupped her face. He caressed her cheeks with his thumb, wiping away fat tears.

"Why are you crying?"

"Please just kiss me," she begged, tilting her head up toward him. Not one to deny a request like that, especially

from her, Lucas pressed his lips to hers. The saltiness of her tears made this dream more real than any of his others. Could you even taste something in a dream?

"Skye," he whispered against her mouth, shifting to move onto the bed beside her.

Angling his body over hers, he pressed against her and poured every ounce of love he had for her into his kiss. She groaned and arched up into him. Lucas ran his hands through her soft hair, letting himself forget that he was only dreaming. Here, at least, she was still his, and he had no intention of letting an opportunity to show her how much he loved her slip through his fingers.

He pulled back and rested his forehead against hers. Hot breath hit his face, adding yet another layer of reality to this dream. He'd take all he could where she was concerned. Seeing her, even if only in his sleep, was the only thing keeping him going.

"I don't know how to find you," he confessed, his voice tortured.

"I'm right here," she insisted as she lifted her face back to his.

He kissed her again, tasting the faintest hint of copper. Pulling back, he brushed his thumb over her lips. When he drew his hand away, his thumb was smeared with blood.

Lucas rolled off of her and watched in growing horror as her eyes rolled back in her head.

"Skye?"

He shook her, but she didn't say a word. Instead, her body convulsed, and Lucas rolled her onto her side as more blood leaked out from the corner of her mouth.

"Skye!"

She began to fade away, and Lucas tried to wrap his arms around her, to keep her here with him, but she was already gone.

LUCAS HIT THE FLOOR WITH A *THUD* AND SAT UP SO abruptly spots appeared in his vision. *What the fuck was that?*

Jumping to his feet, Lucas ran into the living room and let out a breath of relief to see Giles, still sitting on the couch, black book in his lap.

"What has ye in a huff?" the old man asked, looking up through round glasses.

"I want to work more on tracking magic. I think Skye might be in trouble."

"If she's with the Druid, ye can bet yer arse she's in trouble."

CHAPTER 7

SKYE

Skye rolled over and emptied the contents of her stomach. Which, at the moment, were nothing but stale bread and water. Not that it did anything to lessen the painful cramping in her abdomen as she heaved. When there was nothing left, Skye sat back against the wall and wiped her mouth with the back of her hand.

"Ouch!" Pain shot through her hand and radiated up through her arm. *Fuck, fuck, fuck.* Her arm no longer looked broken and wasn't hanging limply from her shoulder. *So, why does it hurt?* Twisting it around, she continued to inspect it. There was no bruising or swelling that she could see, and when she tried to flex it, her arm responded. Still, it sure as hell felt broken.

Fucking asshole. So, what? He'd healed her but left the pain? *What a fucking prince.*

She cradled her arm against her chest and leaned back, closing her eyes. Lucas swam back into her vision, sending tears spilling down her cheeks.

The dream had felt so real. She'd been able to feel

Lucas' warm breath against her skin, and the heat of his hands as they cupped her face so tenderly.

Why did I leave the damn note? Why couldn't I have just gone with them that day? I could've read the journals once we'd gotten back!

Lucas would have come for her if only she'd trusted in what they had, and in what they could have been. Instead, Skye had allowed fear to rule her. She'd believed she was doing Lucas a favor by removing herself from the equation, but all she'd done was ensure the vision she'd Seen would come to be.

Letting out a frustrated breath, Skye squeezed her eyes closed. She knew better. Her visions always came true. Why had she been so sure that leaving would have changed anything?

"So stupid," she muttered in a barely audible voice.

Now, she was going to die, and the Druid would use her death to destroy the man she loved. Leaving hadn't changed a damn thing.

Skye whimpered. Her entire body ached as if she'd been hit by a truck, which she guessed was a fairly accurate description of what had happened to her. How was she supposed to fight for her life when the bastard kept attacking her until she was unconscious?

There was no way for Skye to fight back. For the first time in her life, she was utterly and completely helpless, and the bastard fucking knew it. Not only did he know it, he exploited it.

Light streamed in through the dirty windows, and Skye glanced around her room. The Druid had been busy. Not only had he healed her, but nearly every wall of her prison was now covered in runes she didn't recognize.

There was a scuffle on the other side of the room, and Skye twisted her head to the side. She wasn't alone.

The Druid's black soulless eyes landed on her face. "Good, you're awake."

Skye looked away as he knelt before her and trailed a long finger along her jaw.

"Tell me, Seer, what do you dream of?"

Skye jerked her head away from his unwanted caress, but he gripped her jaw and pulled her back to him, forcing her to meet his gaze.

"None of your business," she snapped.

Her dreams were the one thing that were still hers and hers alone. At least for now. She wasn't about to grant him access to that final piece of her soul.

"You're a tough one, I'll give you that. But still… I'm curious." His fingers left her face and trailed down her throat toward her chest. "You really do make the sweetest sounds when you sleep."

He continued moving his fingers over the swell of her breasts, and Skye closed her eyes as angry tears slipped out from the corners.

"Do you dream of him?"

Skye clenched her jaw, bile rising in her throat. *I wish I could puke on demand. Maybe then he'd think twice before touching me.*

"I bet you do," the Druid continued, musing as he rose to his feet and moved over to the folding chair in the center of the room.

Hearing the soft whisper of his footsteps against the

brick, and feeling the oppressive weight of his presence fade, Skye let her eyes open and turned her attention back to the rune-decorated walls.

"Admiring my work, Seer?"

Unable to contain her curiosity, Skye reluctantly asked, "What is it?"

The Druid clicked his tongue. "I'll share my secrets when you start to share yours."

When Skye remained silent, despite his probing stare, he sighed and got to his feet again. She tracked his movement as he walked to one of the walls. After dipping his finger into what looked like red paint, he began drawing more symbols on the bricks.

"I have plans, Seer. Big plans that involve getting that pathetic grandson of mine out of the way."

"Why? Why can't you just leave him the fuck alone?"

He turned to face her, his eyebrows lifted in a poor imitation of sincere confusion. "If I do that, how will I ever achieve my goals? My future depends on my draining every drop of blood from both him and his sister. The other one I'll play with just for fun. It's the least I can do to the annoying little pest for sticking his nose where it doesn't belong."

Skye's chain rattled as she began shaking with rage. "You're a fucking monster."

He shrugged. "You see me as a monster, but I believe *visionary* is a more apt description."

"Fuck you and your logic. Visionaries don't slaughter innocent people."

"Don't they? I can think of a handful off the top of my head." The Druid laughed and shook his head. "And what of you, darling Seer? How many innocent lives were snuffed out because you never informed them of their fates? Is that not the same as you condemning them to their deaths?"

"That's different."

"Is it?" He tilted his head before his lips curled into a cruel smile. "I'm not sure I agree. Seems to me you might as well have been the one holding the metaphorical scissors that cut the threads of their lives."

To hear her darkest fears spoken out loud by the most depraved being she'd ever met cut more deeply than she'd ever admit. Even still, Skye managed to lift her chin and snarl, "I saved Lizzie from you."

He laughed, a deep belly laugh that rolled through the empty room like thunder. "Oh Seer, you merely delayed my plans. Besides, sparing the life of one does nothing to absolve you from the others."

Still chuckling as if Skye was the most amusing little toy he'd ever played with, the Druid returned to his runes. Once he finished, he made his way back to the folding chair. He sat in it as if it were a throne, and this old warehouse his castle.

Her lip curled with disgust. She hated how entitled he acted, as if he owned everything and everyone. *Just wait until your grandson finds you, you miserable bastard, and you'll see just how wrong you are.*

"Since you seem to want to talk today, how about you tell me what *amria* means?"

Defiance was her only weapon against him. Even though it was futile, Skye let her voice drop to her most threatening whisper. "Even if I knew, I would never tell you."

The Druid's obsidian eyes narrowed. "Do you have any idea what I could do to you?" he hissed. "How many times I can break every single bone in your body, then repair them to start again? You are a blank canvas for me, Seer."

He rose to his feet, and Skye plastered her back against the wall, hot tears already slipping down her cheeks. She turned her head away, refusing to look at him. It was a defensive move more than a spiteful one, Skye didn't want him to see how much his threat terrified her.

"You will answer every single question I have or I will make you beg for death. In fact, the idea of you begging for anything thrills me so much I might have to do it anyway."

Skye's breaths came out in ragged gasps as her heart began to pound. She braced herself for whatever fresh hell he was about to unleash.

The Druid knelt before her and tore her shirt the rest of the way so it hung in two halves, baring the red bra beneath.

She squeezed her eyes shut as his hot breath fanned her face.

"How about we try that again?" he purred in her ear.

"I. Don't. Know," she gritted out, her tears stripping her of any remaining shred of dignity.

He leaned forward and licked away one of the salty drops. "Such beautiful tears," he crooned, then he sighed and pushed to his feet. "Why do you make me hurt you,

Skye? Do you not see how much easier this would be for you if you would only cooperate?"

Without waiting for an answer, in one lightning fast move, he lifted his knee up to his chest and slammed his booted foot down on her face.

There was a crack as her jaw bone shattered, and Skye let out a garbled scream as agony ripped through her. "Please! I don't know!"

Or at least that's what she tried to say. The words were barely recognizable as they left her lips. Apparently, the Druid had no trouble understanding her; he must be fluent in torture victim.

"Lies!" he yelled, and kicked her again, this time in the ribs. Bones snapped beneath his booted foot, and her vision swam.

Skye rolled to the side and, for a moment, there was no pain. In the corner of the room, Lucas stood, eyes blazing like twin beacons calling her home.

She reached for him, and the rest of the world faded away.

WHEN SKYE CAME TO, NIGHT HAD FALLEN. HER BODY ached, but the bones that the Druid broke were once again healed. It was impossible to tell how long she had been out this time; it could have been hours or days.

The Druid stood with his back to her, painting more runes on the wall. A large bundle near his feet drew her attention. She gasped as she met the wide eyes of a man who'd been bound and gagged.

"Your passing out is getting tedious," the Druid told her without turning around. "It's wasting valuable time."

"I'm sorry to be such an inconvenience," she snapped.

"You won't be for much longer. I'm nearly ready for my family reunion."

Skye's eyes widened. How long had she been out?

"I went ahead and picked up my last ingredient while you were sleeping," he said almost conversationally. Turning slightly, he kicked the man, who let out a muffled grunt.

"What do you need him for when you have me?"

The Druid laughed. "Your death will be my grand finale, Seer. He is merely the appetizer."

Horrified, Skye stared into the man's pleading brown eyes. It was bad enough taking the brunt of the psychopath's sadistic tendencies, but it was infinitely worse having to watch it happen to someone else.

"Please just let him go. Use me instead," she begged.

The Druid spared her a glance. "I find it very interesting that you are so eager to give up your life for that of a stranger."

"He's innocent."

"Is he?" The Druid's eyes shifted to the man at his feet. "You sure about that?"

Skye stared at him, then back down at the man. "He doesn't deserve to die."

"You seem awfully certain of his innocence. How do you know he's never done anything to deserve this?"

"No one deserves to be slaughtered."

"You really ought to be more thankful, Seer. This one's death is a gift. It will give you a chance to see my grandson one last time." Lifting the man by his arms, the Druid dragged him toward the north most wall.

"No!" Skye screamed.

The Druid closed his eyes and began chanting over the man's body. He reached down with a blade and cut the man's hands free, pressing one of them against a rune.

"Stop!" Skye screamed. "Let him go!"

The man squirmed, desperate to get free. Even from her perch on the floor, Skye saw the whites of his eyes as he stared at her in total panic. He reminded her of a terrified bunny staring down the barrel of a hunter's gun. At the sound of his muffled screams, Skye struggled to push to her feet, desperate to help him.

The Druid was completely oblivious, wholly focused on whatever dark ritual he was performing. He held his captive against the wall and continued to chant.

The man's screams grew more frantic, and Skye's stomach rolled as the stench of burning flesh filled the room. His arm caught fire first, and Skye watched in horror as the rest of his body quickly followed, turning him into a pillar of dancing flame.

Skye screamed and begged for the Druid to spare the man's life, but the bastard studied her, a small smile playing about his lips. Whatever else the Druid was up to, this was very much a show for her benefit. He wanted her to watch, to see what fate awaited her once he finally decided she'd outlived her usefulness. Skye bit down on her lip, trying to contain her screams as she realized how much he enjoyed them.

After the man crumpled to the ground, nothing more

than a smoldering heap of ash and bone, the Druid stepped toward her.

Skye pushed herself back against the wall as best she could and curled her legs against her chest. "Why did you do that?"

He knelt before her and pulled a sharp blade from his robe. "Great power requires great sacrifice, Skye."

Eyes wide, Skye stared at the blade, instantly recognizing it from her vision. Despite knowing she was completely powerless, she was still determined to fight for her life. She lifted her eyes from the blade and back to his sneering grin.

"You going to kill me now?"

"Not yet, I still have use for you." He waved a hand and both her arms shot out to the side. Another wave, and her legs straightened. As useless as a puppet, Skye sat pinned against the wall, unable to move as the Druid lifted half her tattered shirt, revealing the rune he'd carved into her skin.

"Runes truly are remarkable, aren't they, Seer?"

Skye took advantage of the only power she still held over her body and slammed her eyes closed as the cool blade ran across her skin.

"One small flick of the wrist, and it becomes something new entirely."

The blade bit into her skin, and Skye cried out.

"There we go," he said with a grin. "Now, it will only be a matter of time."

He released her, and Skye glanced down to see a small line carved into the corner of the rune. Warm blood dripped down her side and added itself to the smeared pools she'd already left on the concrete.

Forcing herself to look away, she swallowed back a wave of nausea. Pressing a hand against her side, she gasped around the searing pain, "A matter of time before what?"

He simply stared at her as if she should already know the answer before turning away.

If his plan was to lure Lucas and then kill her, she might as well already be dead. Tired of being a victim in this bastard's game, Skye sneered. "Lucas is going to slaughter you, you worthless piece of shit."

The Druid whirled on her, his face twisting with rage. "Me? What about you, *Seer?* The only power you possess is to bear witness to death that you cannot stop. Nothing you offer is worth anything, and yet you say *I* am worthless?"

He closed the distance between them faster than her eyes could track, simultaneously crouching down and cocking his arm back. His hand cracked across her cheek, and her head slammed back into the bricks. Stars exploded in her vision, each tiny supernova bringing a new wave of molten pain. Skye didn't think her brain could handle many more of these blows, no matter what twisted magic he used to piece her back together. Her body was covered with invisible scars, the remembered pain lingering even after her injuries faded.

Spitting blood on the floor, Skye tilted her chin up defiantly. "Then I guess we're both worthless. Lucas, though, is anything but."

"We will see, won't we?"

Reaching down, the Druid used magic to release her chains. He lifted her by an arm and began dragging her across the floor. She struggled violently, panic chasing her pain, but all the frantic movements did was tear open more of her skin where it rubbed against the ground.

"Where are you taking me?"

"I want you to have a great view of the show, Seer. It's going to be a good one."

He hauled her through the doorway and down a barely lit hall. The farther they got from the room that had been her cell, the more terrified she became.

Lucas would come for her, guns blazing. No matter how angry or hurt he was by her words, he was too good of a man to risk the Druid hurting her. *If he only knew…*

Certain of his victory, Lucas might not consider the fact that it was a trap and she was the bait. If that was the case, there was a very real possibility that the man she loved was going to die.

Tonight.

CHAPTER 8

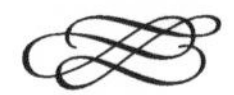

LUCAS

Lucas rocketed out of his chair, sending it flying back into the wall behind him. He pressed his fingers to his temples with an agonized groan as a fresh wave of pain rolled through him. He'd been combing through maps, trying to figure out where his grandfather might be hiding Skye, when sweat had started to drip down his face. That was concerning since he'd hardly been exerting himself, but before he could even process what was happening, a searing pain started to simmer just below his skin. It was like his blood started to boil and set him on fire from the inside out.

On its own, that was already more than enough of a mind fuck, but even so it was only the easier to explain half of what was happening to him. On top of feeling like a human inferno, blinding pain tore through his mind, one endless roar that was drowning out everything else.

He couldn't breathe. It hurt to suck in air, even as his lungs ached for it. Each new breath felt like a living flame burning its way through his tortured body.

As quickly as the sensation started, it vanished, leaving little aftershocks of pain but also glorious emptiness in his mind. If he hadn't still been mostly upright in the middle of the kitchen, Lucas would have sworn he'd just been burned alive. Was this some new present from his asshole grandfather? It was the only explanation for why he could still feel the anguish of the death as if it had been his own.

"What the hell, man?" Matthews shouted, trying to pull the papers he'd been skimming out of the way of the coffee Lucas knocked over. The dark liquid was already soaking the table and everything on it.

Lucas stared down at his hands, trying to put into words the strange sensation that overtook him. *Panic, terror, pain.* He could feel each emotion as if it were him experiencing it. An image of a bloody Skye popped into his head, and Lucas stumbled back against the counter.

"Lucas!" Lizzie cried out, jumping to her feet as she tried to steady him.

"Skye," he wheezed as bone-chilling terror filled him.

Lizzie's eyes widened. "Skye? What's going on, Lucas?"

Matthews moved around the table to stand on the other side of him.

"I can feel her."

"What do you mean you can *feel* her?" Lizzie released him and straightened.

Lucas shook his head, trying to push back the feelings that weren't his own. "I don't know how to explain it," he said, pinching the bridge of his nose. "I can *feel* what she's feeling right now."

"How is that possible? Were you trying out a new

spell?" Lizzie scanned his face as she sought to make sense of his words.

"No, I mean, I was thinking about her, but I wasn't actively trying to find her."

"We need to call Giles," Matthews decided, standing up to grab the phone from the counter.

"What is she feeling?" Lizzie asked.

Lucas looked at his sister. "Terrified. And in a hell of a lot of pain."

Lizzie gasped, her hand flying up to cover her mouth. "Do you think he's going to kill her?"

"He won't. At least not until he gets to me first." Lucas' words were grim but certain. If nothing else, he was sure of that.

"Giles is down the street, he was already on his way over," Matthews informed them, taking his seat back at the table.

As if he hadn't spoken, Lizzie continued with her interrogation. "Do you think you can use whatever it is you're feeling to find out where she is?"

The idea sparked a welcome flare of hope. Lucas closed his eyes and tried to picture Skye. Bright whiskey eyes, dark hair, a smile that lit up any room she entered. He focused on everything he loved about her and tried his best to pinpoint where her fear was coming from. Searing pain shot through his entire body, and Lucas' knees buckled, he had to place both of his hands on the table just to remain standing. All of her suffering, and every bit of her terror, barreled into him like a freight train. Whatever she'd been going through, it was something no person should ever experience.

"Fuck!" Frustration coursed through him as he opened his eyes with a defeated growl. "I can't see anything about where she is." He began to pace.

Lizzie stood and wiped the spilled coffee off the table before turning to pour her brother a fresh cup. She placed the steaming mug in front of him.

The door opened with a crash, and Giles rushed in, red-faced. "What do ye know?"

"Not much," Lucas admitted. "I know she's alive, terrified, and in pain." He ground his teeth together. *The fucking bastard is going to pay for hurting her.*

"How did ye sense her?"

"I don't know. I was sitting there reviewing some maps and drinking coffee and she just popped into my head. Well, first it felt like I was being burned alive, *then* I could feel her."

Giles made a face at Lucas' description.

"What?" Lizzie sputtered. "You didn't mention anything about that part. Don't you think that was a pretty big detail to leave out, *Detective*?"

She used the title with so much sass and exasperation that he couldn't help but think of all the times Skye had done the same.

Giles began to pace, his clipped steps mirroring Lucas' own. "Ye weren't actively trying to find her?"

Lucas shook his head.

"It's a trap. It has to be. He had the lass blocked until he wanted ye to find her." Giles removed his glasses and pinched the bridge of his nose. His green eyes were bright when they met Lucas'. "Ye can't trust the instinct to go to her, not yet. As hard as it is, ye have to ignore it."

"I don't give two shits whether it's a trap or not. I'm going after her," Lucas insisted, anger rising in his chest.

"We," Lizzie automatically corrected.

Lucas shot her a grateful smile before glaring back at the old man.

"I'm not suggesting we leave her to the wolves, but we have to be smart about it. If ye go now, the only thing ye guarantee is a quick death."

"Alright, fine. So, what's your smart plan, Giles?" Matthews snapped. "No matter how we approach this, we're all dangling at the end of that sick bastard's mercy."

"We leave her there much longer and she's the one that's going to die." Lucas folded his arms across his chest. "That's not an option, as far as I'm concerned. So, fine, we account for it being a trap and plan from there. Either way, I'm not wasting any more fucking time. We're doing this."

Giles narrowed his eyes on Lucas' face. "Ye aren't strong enough, lad. He's had decades to cultivate his power. Ye've had days."

"Maybe, but didn't you say we share the same amount of power? It's split between us as the last remaining Druids, right? He's not as powerful as he thinks; everyone's got a weakness. Besides, I have something he doesn't, and no amount of power in the world is going to change that."

"And what's that?" Giles asked.

"You guys. I have a team; he's alone."

"That's great for sentiment, but in terms of an actual fight, ye know as well as we do that we won't be adding much assistance."

Giles ran a hand through his thinning brown hair,

causing it to stand on end. He looked like a flustered hamster in a tweed vest. Definitely not the kind of man Lucas would think to bring with him in a fight, but Giles' knowledge made him a powerful, albeit infuriating, ally.

"Listen, I've made my stance clear, we're going after Skye whether you're in or not. Since you are still huffing from running over here, I can't help but assume you want to help us. So, do it. *Help* me. Help me beat him. Help me get my girl back," Lucas begged, his voice earnest and thickening with the emotion he was trying so hard to keep in check.

Giles narrowed his eyes at Lucas, his stern face softening slightly around the eyes after a moment. "Ye'll get yourself killed. What good will ye be to her then?"

"I'm not arguing with the fact that this is a trap. All I'm asking is that you help us plan around it. Is there anything you can tell us that might give us the upper hand? Any idea about what might be waiting for us?"

The Scot's face fell, his eyes going glossy with unshed tears. "We all know what's waiting for ye," he finally said, his voice defeated. "It's the same thing everyone who goes up against this bastard finds: death."

"WELL, THAT WAS HELPFUL." LIZZIE STEPPED OUT ONTO the back porch and joined Lucas in one of the large wooden armchairs.

"Tell me about it," he responded dryly.

"What are we going to do?"

"I don't fucking know, Lizzie. We go after her, we

might fail, leaving her in his hands forever, but if we don't go, she'll die."

"Sounds like a win-win, if I've ever heard one."

Lucas glanced at his sister, who was doing her best to cheer him up. She hadn't bothered getting dressed yet, and still wore her pajamas. Blonde hair hung down in loose waves, framing her face in a way that made her look more like a teenager than the adult she was.

"Look, you're Lucas fucking MacConnell. You always come out on top, so why can't we tap into some of that arrogance that annoys me and make this work?"

Lucas let out an empty laugh. "I wish it were that easy, but it's not just my life at stake, Lizzie. If I fail, you all die."

His sister patted his arm gently. "Let us worry about our own lives, Lucas. The bottom line is that we have to get Skye. We can't leave her to face that guy all by herself."

Despite her forced bravado, Lizzie's eyes filled, and a fat tear rolled down her pale cheek.

Lucas' heart clenched. He wasn't the only one hurting. Sighing, Lucas covered her hand with his. "I know that. I just need to find out how to do this so we come out with the least amount of collateral damage."

CHAPTER 9

SKYE

It took a moment for Skye to recognize the living room. Only two lights were on, but they shone through the hallway, casting oddly elongated shadows against the floor. Once her eyes adjusted, she rose and walked around the couch, curious about the sprawl of paper and maps on the table. Before she could dip down to inspect them, the soft murmur of voices pulled her focus.

"Lucas, you have to get some sleep."

"We've been over this, Lizzie. I'm not sleeping until I find her."

Drawn to him like a moth helplessly pulled to the flickers of a flame, Skye followed the sound of his voice. When she found him, he was sprawled in a chair on the patio, a mostly empty glass of scotch at his side.

His jaw was coated with the day's stubble, and his hair looked like he'd ran his hands through it more than a few times. Deep purple smudges spoke to the state of his exhaustion and darkened the blue of his eyes, turning them a deep shade of violet. Any other time, it would have been a devastatingly beautiful effect. That was, if they weren't also bloodshot and if the look in them wasn't utterly tortured.

Her superhero was hurting. Worse, he was losing hope.

The need to comfort him overwhelmed her, and Skye drifted closer.

As if he could sense her, Lucas glanced over his sister's shoulder and stared hard at the place Skye stood. She froze, hope and anticipation making her heart flutter wildly in her chest.

He frowned deeply, his brows knitting together.

"Lucas," his sister called, pulling his attention back to her. "Seriously, you're no good to her drunk or exhausted. You can barely keep your eyes open. Go to bed. We can pick this up in the morning."

"Fuck off, Lizzie."

She scowled and crossed her arms, not backing down. Skye smiled even as her heart ached. It was such a typical Lizzie reaction.

"I should have figured this out by now... she's counting on me. We can't just leave her there."

"Lucas." His sister's voice was gentle, even mildly apologetic. "You don't even know where there *is."*

Lucas glowered, his eyes heating with a hint of his power. When he spoke again, his voice was barely more than a growl. "This is what I do, Lizzie. I solve the unsolvable cases. I always catch my guy. I have done this a hundred times for a hundred families. This time, I need a win for me.*"*

"Oh, Lucas," Skye murmured, tears filling her eyes.

If this was a dream, it was cruel. These stolen moments

were all she had to break up the monotony of torture and pain that filled her waking hours. If it was a vision, why was she seeing it? To see how badly her friends were suffering? That they had no clue where to start the search to find her? That she had royally fucked up by not going with them that day? She didn't need that last reminder; it ate at her every waking moment of every day they were apart.

The changes in her gift caused nothing but confusion. It made relying on what she was Seeing and the accuracy of the details impossible. She could no longer tell the difference between visions and dreams because she wasn't familiar enough with the nuances to understand them.

A frustrated huff left her lips. Even if she was no help to them, at least she could see them.

Skye took the last remaining steps that separated her from the chair Lucas sat in. Without conscious thought, she lifted her hand and ran it along his hair, loving the feel of it beneath her fingers.

Lucas froze.

"Lucas?" Lizzie asked, her eyes concerned. "Is it happening again?"

Skye couldn't see his face from where she was standing, but she could hear the wonder in his voice as he whispered her name.

"Skye?"

"I'm here, baby. I'm with you."

When he didn't speak again, it was obvious he hadn't heard her.

His shoulders dropped, his head falling forward. His

heartache was evident in the quivering of his indrawn breath.

It was too much.

Skye bent down and threw her arms around him. "Don't give up. Please. I can't keep fighting him if I know you aren't out there doing the same. I know I don't deserve it, but please don't give up on me."

Lucas tensed, his muscles turning to rock.

He may not have been able to hear her, but he could feel *her.*

Pressing her lips to every inch of his face, she peppered him with ghostly kisses.

Lucas lifted a shaking hand, reaching for the place her face curled into his neck.

"Lucas, you're scaring me!" Lizzie cried out, her voice bordering on hysteria.

He ignored her.

"Skye," he whispered, turning his face toward hers.

The thought of him knowing she was here with him was too irresistible to ignore. Skye ran her nose along the length of his and pressed her lips against his.

"I love you," she whispered as his mouth opened in a surprised o. *"I'm so sorry I tried to leave you." She kissed him again. "Please don't give up on me," she repeated, her voice no more than a broken whisper.*

She watched his throat bob as a sliver of moisture collected in his eyes.

"Skye, if you can hear me," he started, his voice hoarse, "I'm coming for you, baby. Hold on, okay? I'm going to find you, and when I get there, I am going to kill that fucker for what he's done to you. And then, after we

get home, you have some explaining to do, but you'll do it in our bed, while you're in my arms, because I won't let you out of my sight again."

She sobbed as he spoke, her body shaking with the force of her tears as she held onto him. "You've got it, Detective Loomis. Whatever you say. Just get here."

The light began to fade, and Skye only had a matter of seconds left with him. Not knowing if there'd be another chance, she kissed him again, praying with every fiber of her being that he would feel it and know that she was with him.

That she loved him.

When she opened her eyes, he was gone.

THE TEARS WERE STILL WET STREAKS ON HER FACE WHEN she woke up. The Druid had dragged her to some other room, one he obviously spent more time in. There was a cot he'd been sleeping on, if the blankets and pillows were any indication, as well as a desk with a thick tome, runes scrawling across its pages.

The chair, with its ripped vinyl and broken spring, was currently empty, and for that she was grateful. She didn't think she could muster the courage to fight him right now. Her heart was raw, torn open by the sight of a grieving Lucas.

It was one thing to feel her own heartbreak and have to learn to live with it. It was another thing entirely to witness the full impact of what her absence had done to the man she loved, to know what that kind of devastation looked like. There was no unseeing it. And the knowledge hurt worse than any vision of death she'd ever experienced.

The door swung open with a crash, and Skye jerked upright.

"It would seem we have both misjudged my grandson, Seer."

To say the Druid was displeased would have been the grossest of understatements. His black eyes had a red glow, and his lips were twisted in a sneer.

"Either he is truly incompetent," he continued, "or we overestimated his attachment to you."

She'd Seen the truth for herself, but still, the words stung.

Not waiting for her reply, he stepped toward his desk and began to rifle through the pages. "I know he felt you. He should be drawn to your beacon. What could possibly be keeping him?"

Dragging a finger along one of the pages, the Druid let out a soft "ah" that left Skye trembling. There was entirely too much pleasure in the sound.

"Perhaps he just needs a little more incentive. What do you think, Seer? Should we send my grandson a gift?"

His eyes trailed along her body, and Skye felt like spiders were crawling along the length of her. She began shaking in earnest.

"Let's start off small. It needs to get his attention, but not completely ruin your charm." The Druid chuckled. "In the end, it doesn't really matter. Although, if he finds you too disfigured, he may not think you're worth saving."

He reached for her hand, and Skye spit in his face.

He flicked his eyes up to hers, and the look he gave her

was so full of menace, she knew she'd just witnessed evil in its purest form.

"When will you learn, Seer?" he crooned, a dagger flashing in his hand.

Where did that come from? Skye pressed herself back, trying to escape him, but it was too late. Her pitiful act of defiance had stripped away the last piece of his sanity. If he'd even had any to begin with.

"N-no," she whimpered. "Please."

She'd gotten used to his games, but he'd never looked at her like this. And if he wanted to send Lucas a present, that sounded a lot more permanent than what he'd been doing.

"A little souvenir, I think," he murmured, dragging the cool blade along her cheek in the most twisted imitation of a caress.

She began babbling, nonsensical words leaving her in a rush.

"Shhh," the Druid whispered, the dagger lifting up off her skin.

Skye knew better than to hope. There was no escaping this.

When his wrist slashed down, she flinched, but he'd once again used his power to hold her in place. His blade struck true, and sticky warmth trickled down the side of her neck, but she was too numb to do more than stare at the bloodied piece of flesh in his outstretched hand.

Shock took over, protecting her in the only way it could.

Her ear. The bastard had cut off her ear.

"A little token for the both of you. Fitting, really.

Maybe now you'll learn how to listen. Or at the very least, obey."

The shock began to fade, and Skye let out her first bloodcurdling scream as searing pain tore through her head. With a final sneer, the Druid left her to her horrified screams.

CHAPTER 10

LIZZIE

"Skye, no! Please, don't leave! Skye!" Lucas jumped out of his chair, spinning in a circle as he searched every inch of the kitchen. "Come back!" he called, frantically checking for the ghost of Skye that haunted him.

Lizzie watched, completely helpless, as her big brother, the one man who had always been braver and more together than anyone else she'd ever known, completely broke down. She hadn't ever seen him fall apart like this. Not even when their parents died.

Lucas fell back into his chair, head falling into his hands as he began to sob uncontrollably. His entire body shook with the force of his tears. He was muttering something, but the words were unintelligible. Not once in their entire lives had she ever seen him look so fragile.

Clearing her throat and trying unsuccessfully to contain the emotion inside of her, Lizzie rushed to his side, wrapping her arms around his shaking shoulders in a desperate attempt to comfort him.

"Lucas, what's wrong?"

It was obvious some of his Druid mojo had allowed him to connect to Skye, but for her part, it just looked like her brother had spent the better part of five minutes talking to a ghost. If he'd been anyone else, she would have assumed he belonged in a psych ward.

"She was here. I felt her, Lizzie."

"And could you hear her?" she asked hesitantly, not sure which answer she was hoping for.

"No, damn it!"

"Shhh, it's okay. If she is still strong enough to find a way to connect with you, then it means she's still alive and fighting." Lizzie sat down on the small table and faced her brother. "What do you need to find her? If your detective skills aren't working, what else can we try?"

Lucas' head shot up, his red-rimmed eyes meeting hers with panic that bordered on desperation. "I don't know? Don't you think I've tried everything already?"

"Unless you're ready to give up, that means we need to think of something you haven't tried," she told him matter-of-factly.

He stared at her helplessly. "I don't know what to do."

"You have all this power now, surely there's some kind of spell that can help you track someone down."

Lucas shook his head. "We already tried that. Giles and I—"

"You tried that *before*. Didn't Giles say that the Druid broke whatever spell was blocking you from finding her? Maybe you just need to try again."

Hope blossomed in his eyes, and Lucas pushed himself out of his chair. "I can't believe I didn't think of that," he muttered, already walking toward the door. "Giles!" he bellowed.

Lizzie shook her head, as he walked out of the kitchen. "You're welcome," she called after him with a sigh.

He might have completely forgotten she was there, but at least he'd stopped crying. That was the kind of win she could feel proud of. It might be a small one in the scheme of things, but right now, her brother had newfound hope and a plan. Two things he desperately needed.

Now, all they could pray for was that he found Skye so they could bring her back home.

James came into the room a few seconds after Lucas disappeared. "Hey, beautiful," he started, but stopped, his smile faltering as he rushed to her. "What's wrong? What happened?"

Lizzie shook her head, not sure she could find the words without completely losing it. She'd managed to help Lucas gain some hope, but her own was disappearing every day that passed leaving them no closer to finding Skye.

"Shhhh, baby," James murmured in her ear, pulling her against his body.

Lizzie wrapped her arms around his waist and held on, enjoying the warmth and strength of him.

"Lucas felt her," she finally said, stepping back and wiping her eyes.

James' brow lifted. "What do you mean *felt* her?"

Taking a seat, Lizzie shrugged as James sat next to her, gripping her hand. "I'm not sure. One moment, he was sitting here in all his typical frustrated glory, and the next, he was talking to a—"

"To a what?"

"A ghost?"

James paled. "Does that mean she's dead?"

"I don't think so. Maybe she connected with him somehow? Found a way to reach him?"

James slumped back in his chair. "I know I've said it before, but this is the craziest shit I've ever witnessed."

Lizzie offered a slight smile to the man who managed to make her happy even on the darkest of days. "Same here."

He kissed the top of her hand. "I tell you, I long for the days of secretly checking you out over the diner counter."

"Oh?"

James grinned. "I stole a lot of secret glances," he said with a wink.

"I suppose that makes two of us." Her smile disappeared as the broken image of her brother came back into her mind. "You should have seen him, James. He looked so…fragile. Like one small gust of wind would make him crumple."

James instantly sobered. "Babe, the woman he loves is missing; that's enough to make any strong man fall to his knees. If anything happened to you…I don't know what I would do."

Lizzie scooted her chair closer and leaned against his shoulder. James pressed a kiss to the top of her head, and they sat in silence for a few moments before Lizzie got to her feet.

"I guess we'd better go see if we can help."

"Sounds good to me."

Lizzie turned, about to grab a fresh cup of coffee to

take with her, when she spotted a small box on the counter. "What's that?" she asked. "It wasn't there before, was it?"

"No, I don't think so."

James approached the small box with caution, as if it were a snake about to strike at any moment.

"Then where did it come from?"

"I have no fucking clue."

Grabbing a wooden spoon from a drawer, he gently tapped the box, before scooting it farther onto the counter. When nothing happened, he set the wooden spoon aside and lifted the lid using his index finger and thumb.

Lizzie shuffled closer to his back, standing on her tiptoes to peer over his shoulder and see inside.

"Fucking shit!" he exclaimed, slamming the lid back down.

Harsh buzzing filled her ears, and she swayed back onto her heels. "Oh my God," Lizzie breathed, covering her mouth with her hands as her brain scrambled to process what she'd just seen hidden within the innocent-looking container.

Stomach rolling, she spun toward the trash can with a horrified yelp.

CHAPTER 11

LUCAS

Lucas flew through the house, heading straight to the study where he'd last seen Giles. The Scot was sitting in the same dark green, high-backed chair in the corner he'd been in earlier, his nose buried in a book.

"I want to try again," Lucas said, stepping farther into the room.

Giles looked up, pushing his glasses back up on his nose. "Want to try what?"

"To track her. I think I've been—"

Lucas broke off to search for the words to explain what he'd experienced on the patio. Skye had been there, he knew it. Somehow, she found a way to reach out to him to let him know she was alive. The ball was in his court now, and he'd be damned if he let her down. Finally, he settled on the closest thing to the truth he could think of.

"I've been feeling her."

Giles raised a bushy eyebrow, his eyes owlish behind the golden frames. "*Feeling* her?"

Lucas ran his hands through his hair and down his face. *Shit, I sound crazy.* "I don't know how else to explain it, but she was here, Giles. I know it."

The older man's brows knitted together. "Could it have been the Druid reaching out to ye?"

Lucas thought of the brush of air against his cheeks and lips that reminded him so much of tender kisses, and the tingle on his scalp that always accompanied Skye's fingers running through his hair. The Druid was a determined bastard, but Lucas very much doubted even he would go that far. His forms of torture were more sadistic than emotional.

After a beat, Lucas shook his head decisively. "No way it was him. It was definitely Skye, Giles."

Giles studied him for a moment, his moss-green eyes giving nothing away. After the silence stretched into uncomfortable territory, he shut the book gently and set it on the table beside him. "Very well, let's give this a try."

The older man got to his feet and stretched his back, the series of accompanying cracks and pops testament to the fact that he had been sitting in the same spot for most of the afternoon.

"I've been searching through the book, looking for a tracking rune—"

"And?" Lucas interjected impatiently.

Giles raised a brow. "But I haven't had any luck so far. We'll have to do this just like before. Ye ready?"

"Yes."

Lucas shook out his hands and rolled his neck a few times, trying to force his body to relax. He was running on pure adrenaline, and calming his mind enough to focus on the task at hand was a trial in and of itself. After a few deep breaths, Lucas closed his eyes and focused on his favorite memories of Skye. He imagined running his hands through the silky strands of her dark hair while she slept beside him, the way her eyes lit up when she smiled, the impish way her nose crinkled when she called him Detective. He focused as hard as he could on the love between them.

There had to be some power in that.

Minutes ticked by painfully slowly as nothing but the images he created filled his mind. His hands clenched as impatience spread through his body, each muscle tensing with an overwhelming sense of frustration. He opened his mouth to complain—

Pain exploded in his head near his right ear, then shot down his body, sending agony through each limb, into each digit. Lucas gasped, lights exploding behind his eyes at the intensity of the fire raging within his body. He nearly opened his eyes, but he couldn't afford to be distracted, so he concentrated harder, letting the pain envelope him.

"I think it's working," he ground out.

"Good, focus on that feeling. Try to see her, Lucas," Giles told him softly. "What is the source of her pain?"

"It's all over…I can't pinpoint a single spot." He clamped his teeth together, the throbbing ache so powerful it nearly fractured his focus.

As he continued to breathe through the pain, an image began to take shape. It was Skye, lying on the ground, her body shaking as she cried.

"Skye?" he whispered, moving toward her.

She didn't hear him, but he drank in every inch of her.

Lucas' body began to tremble as he took stock of her injuries. Based on what he could see, she'd been beaten—repeatedly. She was bruised and broken, but at least she was alive. Her once white shirt had been nearly shredded and was covered in dried blood.

"Baby, what has he done to you?" Agony laced Lucas' words, and fresh tears splashed his cheeks. "Where are you, Skye?"

Lucas looked for anything that might show him her location, but the room was nearly dark and mostly empty with the exception of a cot, small desk, and an old chair. He turned around slowly, and his lip curled. Behind him was a window made with what looked like one-way interrogation glass.

Stepping toward it, he tried to peer out, but just as he got close enough to maybe see what was outside, a scream radiated through him, and he was pulled from the vision.

"Fuck!" Lucas shouted, beyond frustrated to lose his connection to Skye. "What the hell is going on?"

He looked to Giles for an answer, but the man was staring past him into the hall.

"MacConnell!" Matthews yelled. "You need to come see this! Now!"

"What is it?" Lucas called back, torn between trying again and seeing what the commotion was about.

"Now, damn it!" Matthews growled.

Decision made for him, Lucas and Giles raced down the hall toward the kitchen, rounding the corner as Lizzie heaved violently into the trash can. Lucas lunged toward his sister, but Giles stopped him.

"I've got her, go."

Lucas turned to Matthews, fully taking in his partner for the first time since entering the room. He stood, hands on his hips, looking like he was seconds away from joining Lizzie. His face was beet red and twisted in a mixture of agony and rage.

Panic sent Lucas' heart stuttering within his chest. "What is it?"

Matthews pointed to a small box on the counter. Lucas stared at it in confusion. How could a tiny box cause such extreme reactions?

The box was small—maybe large enough to fit a softball inside—and was made of dark mahogany. It was old, scratched, and looked completely harmless, but Lucas knew better. Nothing good could be in there. The real question was: how bad was it?

Swallowing hard, Lucas stepped forward.

Lifting the box carefully, Lucas removed the lid. The tremor in his hand intensified and all coherent thought fled his mind. He stumbled, the lid falling from his hand as he reached for the counter to help keep himself upright. He gagged on a wave of nausea, nearly losing the contents of his stomach right there.

He practically threw the box, sending it skidding across the countertop. He didn't need to look inside again. The image of what sat there would haunt him for the rest of his life.

A bloody ear rested on top of a piece of what had once been white fabric. He didn't need the shooting star earring to tell him who it belonged to. The pain he'd felt while trying to reach for Skye made sense now. He'd experienced the exact moment the fucker mutilated her.

Hands clenched into fists, Lucas reached for the power that pulsed in time with his heartbeat. With rage unlike anything he'd ever felt before, Lucas pulled his magic up to the surface.

"Where are you, you son of a bitch?" he yelled, focusing on the source of that rage.

The Druid appeared in his mind, as clear as if he stood in the same room, with his trademark smug smile on full display. The empty warehouse he stood in was covered in runes Lucas didn't recognize, but none of that mattered.

"I guess you got my present." The Druid's smile grew as the deep voice reverberated in Lucas' mind. *"Glad I finally got your attention. See you soon, Grandson."*

Lucas opened his eyes, knowing exactly where to find the bastard who'd once been family, and more importantly, where to find Skye.

"I GO IN FIRST. YOU TWO LOOK FOR THE ROOM WHERE Skye is being held. It's in the same building, but not the same room the Druid was in when I saw him," Lucas briefed Giles, Lizzie, and Matthews. "Get her and get the fuck out. You do not come back for me, am I clear?"

"Lucas, you can't expect us to just leave you there!" Lizzie insisted, the stubborn set of her jaw so like his own.

"Yes, I can," he snapped. "You get Skye and get the fuck out. I can't focus if I'm constantly worried about the rest of you."

"I will use Lucas' blood to rune the door so the Druid can't come in, just in case things go sideways."

"Are we seriously planning for you to lose?" Lizzie asked angrily, her eyes blazing as she looked between the three men. "Are you planning on dying tonight, Lucas?"

Matthews reached down and squeezed Lizzie's hand. His time as Lucas' partner meant he knew exactly what Lucas was doing and why. When going after a perp this dangerous, they had to have a backup plan. When things went south—because they most assuredly would—his team had to get as far away from the Druid as possible.

"No, I'm not planning on dying," Lucas replied, folding his arms, "but it would be stupid to go in unprepared. We need to plan for every outcome, Lizzie."

She sniffled, but shed no tears. "Fine. So, we rune the door, and get Skye. How do you expect us to get out without you?"

"We run like hell, Liz," Matthews said, brushing his thumb along the back of her hand. "Get out of that building as quickly as we can and hope Giles' rune holds. That's all we can do."

"I will do what I can with Lucas' blood," Giles explained. "Here's hoping it works."

They hadn't been able to test their theory that his blood would work with runes he didn't paint, but it was the best idea they had. If Lucas lost, he had to believe his blood would be enough to get them to safety.

"Skye's in bad shape. She's going to need help. I'm counting on you guys to take care of her." Lucas stepped forward and pulled his sister in for a hug. "I love you, Lizzie. Please have faith in me."

"I do," she whispered against his chest. "Just don't die."

CHAPTER 12

LIZZIE

Giles parked his car in front of an old warehouse building not even thirty minutes from the cabin. Skye had been so close to them this entire time, and they hadn't even known it. The red brick structure loomed in the darkness, and even from her spot in the car, Lizzie could feel the evil rolling off it in waves. The feeling made her nauseous, and if it hadn't been for James' hand in hers, she would have lost her nerve. Every instinct screamed for her to run.

They were walking into a trap that they may not survive, and each of them knew it. What if they didn't make it back out?

"It will be okay, Liz," James whispered into her ear. "I love you."

"I love you, too," she answered, pressing a kiss to his lips.

Lucas turned to face them, and Lizzie memorized her brother's face. Out of all of them, his chances were the worst.

"You ready?" He searched her gaze.

She shook her head. How could she ever be ready to lose the last remaining member of her family?

"It will be okay, Lizzie," he assured her. "You'll be back to kicking my ass at Candy Land in no time." He smiled.

Lizzie choked out a sob. "I love you, Lucas."

"I love you, too, Lizzie." He shifted his focus to Giles. "Wait five minutes, then come in after me."

"Will do."

Lucas turned back to Lizzie and James. "Do not come after me, no matter what. I will find you."

"You got it, partner," James answered for both of them. "Be careful in there."

"You too. Keep my sister safe."

"With my life."

The men shared a long look before Lucas nodded.

Unable to speak, Lizzie watched her brother climb from the car and disappear inside the dark building. She tried like hell to muffle the voice telling her it was the last time she'd ever see him alive. *He will be fine.* Her brother was the strongest, most determined man she knew, and if there was any hope of winning this battle, it was with him.

Minutes ticked by like hours, but the building remained silent. If there was a war going on inside, no evidence made it out to them.

"Ready?" James squeezed her hand.

Lizzie forced herself to look away from the warehouse and back to him. Nodding, she answered, "Let's do this."

Together, the three of them climbed from the car and made their way inside. The sour stench of mildew hit her nose the second they were within the walls. The bottom floor was empty, except for some trash and a dusty old chair.

James took the lead. Still gripping her hand, he headed for the stairs. Each step they took echoed in her head, although they were nearly silent. Once reaching the landing for the second floor, they resumed their search. Lizzie took a door on the right hall, opening it to find nothing inside but a crumpled-up sheet.

James and Giles must've had the same luck with the rooms they chose because both shook their heads after making their way back to the stairs.

The trio ascended again, to the third and final floor in the building, only just reaching the top when faint voices reached them.

James rushed toward the door directly in front of them and peered through the glass. "Giles, rune this one!" he whispered loudly.

Without questioning him, Giles dipped his finger inside the plastic container holding Lucas' blood and drew a symbol on the steel door.

James turned away and tried the only other door in the hall, cursing when it was locked. Pulling a small kit from his pocket, he went to work picking the lock.

Lizzie turned her attention to the door Giles had just finished working on and stepped up to the glass.

"Don't, lass," Giles said softly, grasping her arm. "He's alive, but ye won't do him any good by going in there now."

Tears burning in her eyes, Lizzie stared helplessly at the door and nodded. He was right. She didn't possess the strength to walk away if she saw her brother losing, and she sure as hell didn't want to be the distraction that led to his death.

Turning her attention back to James, relief flooded her when the lock clicked and he pushed the door open.

"It's her!" he called. Stepping inside, he froze for a moment, then muttered, "Shit."

Abandoning the hall, Lizzie rushed in behind him. The room was small, more of a closet than anything. Skye was tied to a chair facing a darkened pane of glass, where they could see Lucas' back as he faced off with the Druid.

Lizzie's blood iced as she remembered the way the Druid's soulless eyes bore into hers as he told her she was going to die.

"Lizzie, I need your help."

James' voice pulled her from her thoughts, and Lizzie turned back to Skye. He worked on releasing Skye's right hand, while Lizzie untied the rope on her left.

"Skye, can you hear me?" he said in a soothing voice. "Skye?"

Skye's eyes fluttered open. She stared at him, confusion etched on her face. "James?" Her voice was weak and scratchy. "Am I dreaming again?"

"No, sweetheart. We're here."

Skye choked on a sob and leaned forward into James' arms. Lizzie fought back tears of her own, relieved that they'd found her and no one had died yet.

"It's okay, we've got you," James murmured, rubbing his hand in a circular motion on Skye's shaking back.

"Where's Lucas?" she asked, leaning back to look up at his face.

"In there," Giles answered, pointing to the other side of the glass.

"Oh no," she moaned, sagging in James' arms. "We have to warn him! It's a trap!"

"He knows, and he can take care of himself," James said. "We have to get you out of here. We promised him." Without waiting for her response, James lifted her into his arms.

They couldn't hear what was happening on the other side of the glass, but the Druid looked entirely too smug, which didn't bode well for any of them.

Following the Druid's pointing hand, Lucas turned to the glass, and Lizzie watched his eyes widen with terror. *Can he see us?* Her brother narrowed his eyes and turned back to the Druid.

"It's one way," James said, answering her unspoken question. "He can't see in here."

"Oh no," Giles mumbled, almost tripping over his feet as he stepped back from the glass. "No, no, no…"

"What is it?" Lizzie asked, her heartbeat tripling in time as she looked at the old man. His mouth hung open in horror, and the blood had drained from his face.

"We have to get him out of there. I know what those symbols mean!" he shouted, already running to the door. Before he cleared the threshold, blinding light filled the room.

"What the hell is going on?" James asked, cradling Skye's battered body as he turned away from the light.

"Lucas!" Skye screamed, reaching out a bloodied hand toward the glass.

Lizzie spun back to the glass, searching for any sign of

Lucas, but he was gone. The only thing left in the room was the Druid smiling with sinister satisfaction.

Denial and grief spiraled within her. "No!" Lizzie cried as her heart stuttered. Agony ripped through her as she stared at the spot her brother had been only seconds before. "Lucas!"

"We have to go!" James yelled as the Druid made his way toward the glass.

"Hope you enjoyed the show, Seer!" he cried jubilantly.

"Run!" James insisted.

They sprinted out of the room and down the stairs, but Lizzie's legs felt like lead as she ran. She was the worst kind of coward for leaving her brother behind. *You didn't leave him behind, he's already gone.* She stumbled at the reminder, but caught herself and forced her body forward.

"No! We have to go back!" Skye screamed, squirming weakly in James' arms.

"Skye, stop! This is what Lucas wanted!" he yelled back at her.

"No, no, no, no," Skye cried, shaking her head.

Roaring sounded behind them, and Lizzie pushed herself further. If they made it out, maybe they could find a way to save Lucas. But if they died here, he would be gone forever, no maybe about it. That knowledge alone was enough to keep her moving.

They just reached the bottom floor, Giles leading the way. He was no longer concerned with stealth, and he burst through the doors, which clanged loudly against the outer walls of the warehouse. They raced across the street, Skye bouncing in James' arms as she clung to him. Giles had already started the car when Lizzie slammed the door closed behind her.

"What the fuck just happened?" James demanded as soon as they were speeding down the street.

"Lucas is gone," Giles answered, his voice shaking.

Skye let out a choked cry, and Lizzie looked back to where she lay in James' lap.

"What do you mean *gone*?" Lizzie asked, her stomach twisting into knots.

"Is he dead?" James asked, saying the word she'd been actively avoiding.

Giles shook his head, and hope flared back to life within her. If he wasn't dead, that meant they could save him.

"It's worse," Giles replied.

"What the hell is worse than death?"

"The Wasteland," Skye answered, her voice weak and packed with pain.

Lizzie's hope drained from her like a popped balloon.

"What do you mean, the Wasteland?" she asked, even though she already knew the answer.

"The Druid escaped, can't Lucas?" James asked.

They all knew the likelihood of that. It had taken the Druid nearly three decades to escape, and he'd been practiced at his craft beforehand. What were the odds Lucas could do the same?

Lights flew by them as Giles guided the car out of town. Lizzie drowned out the sound of Skye's sobs and focused on the last time she'd seen her brother.

Life without him wasn't an option, but how the hell were they supposed to get him back?

CHAPTER 13

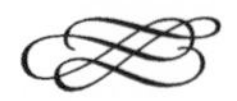

LUCAS

Lucas moved through the building without really seeing, drawn upstairs like a magnet pulled to its other half. Not bothering to question the pull, he followed the impulse, silently moving through the abandoned warehouse, his racing heart his only companion. Reaching the top of the stairs, he opened the first door and stepped inside.

At the far wall, the Druid turned away from a glass window to face him. "It's about time."

"Fuck you."

The Druid laughed, true delight filling the sound. "My, what a passionate one you are. It truly is a shame I must destroy you. It could have been fun training you if it didn't require sharing what is rightfully mine."

Lucas rolled his eyes. "Listen, this whole 'your power belongs to me' thing is getting really old. You're going to kill me, I get it. How about I turn myself over and you let the rest of them go."

"Ah, but where's the fun in that?"

Lucas' hands balled into fists. He worked his jaw, trying to keep his anger in check. Needing to buy the others time to find Skye and get her out of here, he couldn't afford to give in to his rage. At least not yet. "Can't blame a guy for trying," he said with a shrug.

The Druid studied him with narrowed eyes. "You seem to be taking this all very casually for someone who's threatened me with violence at every turn. Have you finally given up?"

Never, you sack of shit. *"I just don't see the point of drawing out the inevitable."*

"I can't say I blame you, although it's not going to change anything for your girlfriend." The Druid cocked his head. "Is she still your girlfriend? When I found her, she was in the middle of leaving you."

Lucas fought to keep his expression neutral, the reminder of Skye's note still holding the power to gut him. "Couples fight. It was a misunderstanding."

"That's a hell of an overreaction to a lovers' quarrel. What did you do?" he asked, moving closer.

Instinct made Lucas side-step, not wanting to allow him to get too close, although the move did pull Lucas away from the door. Not ideal.

With a flick of his wrist, the Druid sent the door slamming shut. "Not like you were getting out of here anyway. Might as well make ourselves comfortable."

Lucas glanced around the empty room. "How do you propose we do that?"

"Nothing wrong with getting to know my grandson, is there?"

He snorted. "So, now I'm your grandson? I think that

ship sailed the moment you decided to murder me and my sister."

"It's not my fault that the power demands your blood. The rules are clear. All living Druids hold equal shares of the power to keep the balance. The only way I can access more is to remove those that stand in my way."

"What about the balance?"

"Balance is for the weak."

Mentally counting the time in his head, Lucas assumed the others must have entered the building by now. That meant he needed to keep this going for another five or ten minutes at least, to ensure that they got back out again. Thankfully, this asshole liked to talk.

"What good is living forever when you have no one to share your life with?" Lucas asked.

A flicker of something crossed the Druid's face, but it was gone before Lucas could identify it. "That was never the plan," he admitted, "but if I must pay that price then I do so gladly."

Thinking of Skye and the future they could have built if this bastard hadn't interfered, Lucas couldn't agree. Nothing in the world would be worth the price of losing the chance to spend his life loving her.

"Maybe you just didn't deserve Nan...I mean, I know there are people out there that would lay down their lives to save me, but I don't think they'd be as willing to do it as a way to get away from me."

Scowling, the Druid advanced. Lucas shadowed each step with one of his own, until his back was facing the oddly placed interior window.

"Enough of this. I grow bored."

"You were the one who wanted to get to know me."

"A mistake I do not care to repeat."

"Hit a nerve, did I?"

"I'll be rid of you soon enough."

The Druid pointed behind him, and an acrid heat licked at his back. Lucas glanced over his shoulder to find that a portal had opened behind him.

No! *It was too soon. The others needed more time.*

"You going somewhere?" Lucas asked, hoping his voice didn't betray his nerves.

The Druid grinned. "No, but you are. Call it a short stay of execution, but it won't last long. I need you out of my way temporarily, and I couldn't think of a better way to make that happen."

Runes flared to life around him, covering the walls and the floor beneath his feet. Lucas tried to step out of the illuminated circle, but slammed into an invisible barrier.

"Too late, Detective. But you knew that as soon as you stepped in here. I promise to take very good care of your Seer once you're gone. I've really enjoyed my time with her."

"Don't you fucking touch her!" Lucas shouted as his mind raced. He wasn't walking out of this, but defeat didn't sit well with him.

Cocking his head, the Druid snickered and waved. "Enjoy your time in the Wasteland. Once I've gotten rid of every other obstacle in my way—"

A roar began to build behind him, and Lucas couldn't hear the rest of what the Druid said. He patted his pockets, searching for something he could use to disrupt the barrier long enough to get himself out of it with a rune of his own.

Purple light radiated out from the runes, growing in strength until Lucas had to shield his eyes from the blast.

Too late. Time was up.

Invisible flames enveloped him, and Lucas screamed.

STILL SCREAMING, HIS BODY ENGULFED BY INVISIBLE flames, Lucas bolted upright, scrambling back on his hands and feet until he realized he was alone. Again. He had no idea how long he'd been here; the light never changed to indicate the passing of days, but this was the fifth time Lucas had relived that fucking night.

The fifth time Lucas had to watch the smile on that smug bastard's face as he was ripped away from everyone that mattered to him.

As always, the feeling of helplessness ate at him. In the end, he'd been no good to any of them. He might have bought them time, but if he was trapped here in the Wasteland, then they were on their own…which meant they were as good as dead.

Dropping his head into his hands, Lucas let out a scream of rage. "Fuck!"

There wasn't even anything to hit, no way to expel the anger inside him. Wasteland was an apt name for this place. Nothing alive—aside from himself—survived here. The entire fucking landscape was a barren sandpit, void of nearly all color. The sky looked like something out of a cartoon, a mix of gray-blue swirls that could have been clouds or even the other side of a portal. Even he was muted here, as if the life that animated him was slowly draining away.

His power sizzled beneath his skin in response to the twin flames of anger and frustration at war within him. He couldn't just sit here and wait to die. With no other option available to him—and sitting still was *not* an option—Lucas began walking. At least, this way, he was moving forward.

If his grandfather found a way out of the Wasteland, he could do the same.

Or he'd die trying.

Chapped lips bled, providing him with the tangy taste of copper as he moved. There was no water, no food, in this nightmarish place. Lucas felt no hunger or thirst, no happiness, nothing but rage and guilt for those he'd left behind to fight his war.

Sand sucked at his feet as he walked, turning his steps into a heavy trudge, but he kept going. Even when it felt like his legs turned to rubber and his lungs burned like they were on fire, no matter what, he had to get to them. Even if it killed him.

Hell, he might as well already be dead.

Lizzie.

Matthews.

Skye.

The thought of her brought a lump to his throat. The Druid had let him know she was alive, but in what shape? He knew the fucker had cut her ear off; what other damage had he done?

Lucas clenched his fists and used the bubbling rage to push himself harder.

A shadow took shape in front of him. It stood far enough away on a sand dune that Lucas couldn't make out anything other than a humanoid form. Hope bloomed in his chest. *Maybe whoever it is knows how I can get the hell out of here!*

"Hello?" he shouted, moving faster. "Hey!" he yelled again, running as fast as his legs would carry him.

The closer he got, the clearer the image became, and it wasn't long before Lucas recognized who was in front of him.

"Skye! Thank God! How did you get here? Are you alright?" He rushed up the dune toward her.

She didn't respond, didn't react in any way to his presence, just stood before him in jeans and a white T-shirt, dark hair braided down her back.

"Are you alright?"

He searched her for injuries, starting with her legs, then slowly letting his gaze travel up her body. He reached her head and clenched his jaw as unease twisted in his belly and grief slid icy fingers around his heart. The woman before him still had both ears.

Lucas would never forget what he'd found in that box.

"You aren't here," he whispered, his voice cracking on the words.

This version of Skye cocked her head to the side, studying him. She reached for him, and he backed away, shaking his head.

"You aren't really here," he repeated, the words damn near choking him with grief. Was she just some figment of his imagination here to torture him? Is that what happened in the Wasteland, just an eternity of psychological torture? He wouldn't survive that.

"Lucas," she whispered.

Lucas shook his head in denial. "Not here…you aren't here!"

She smiled and turned into granules of sand that swirled around him on a small gust of air before falling to the ground, leaving him empty and alone once more.

CHAPTER 14

SKYE

Skye's eyelids fluttered open, and she squinted in the light streaming through the windows.

For a brief moment, she wondered if the last few weeks had been nothing but a nightmare. A horrific, soul-crushing nightmare. She glanced at the door, half-expecting Lucas to walk in, a smug smile on his face. *Just another normal morning...*

But as she woke up, realization ripped that hope away as quickly as it had come, and the facts hit her like a freight train.

Lucas was gone.

He was never coming for her.

She was alone.

Even if the latter wasn't entirely true, since Lizzie, James, and Giles were all in the next room, without Lucas she still felt like it. Life without him seemed empty, now that she understood what living without him would mean.

Skye sat up, her head aching and hot, although the worst of the physical pain had passed. She scratched at the skin just above where her ear had been, the thick bandage making it impossible to relieve the itch entirely. She'd refused to go to the hospital, not wanting to deal with the inquiries a missing limb would necessitate. Whatever magic the Druid had used to hold her steady had also cauterized the wound, so there wasn't much that could be done anyway, other than cleaning it and bandaging her up. James had volunteered, stating he was the only one with any semblance of medical training. Even still, Skye knew it wasn't easy for him, given his aversion to blood.

She'd gotten off lucky, all things considered, the Druid could have done so much worse. Hell, he *had* done worse, night after night. But this time, he hadn't just marked her, he'd taken a piece of her. Permanently. And not just in the physical sense.

The Druid may have chopped a piece of her off, but he shattered her heart by destroying the man she loved.

Getting to her feet, Skye stretched and finally got out of the bed that still smelled like the man she loved. Tears burned in her eyes, the lump in her throat all but choking her, and she staggered. Gripping the headboard for support, Skye forced herself to take a deep breath.

In and out.

Once.

Twice.

It was all she could do to keep herself from falling apart.

Making her way out the door and down the hall, voices carried toward her. Since this was the first time she'd ventured out of her room, Skye used the muffled voices to guide her to the others.

Lucas had been gone for five days. Five miserable, pain-filled, nightmarish days, and she'd slept for most of them.

Although she dreamt of him every time she closed her eyes, it was bittersweet torture Skye wished would let up, if even for a single night. Not that she deserved the peace; his imprisonment was her fault.

The voices grew louder, and Skye turned the corner and found herself in the small kitchen. Lizzie stood at the outdated stove, cooking something Skye had no interest in eating, while James and Giles looked up at her.

At the sudden silence, Lizzie turned around. "Skye!" she said, rushing toward her. "Are you okay? Do you need anything?"

Skye shook her head, the lump in her throat growing larger. She'd seen Lizzie a few times when she'd brought food in, but facing her friend after what she'd been about to do to her brother was nearly too much.

"Are you sure?" Lizzie's face fell. "Honey, it's okay." Lizzie pulled her in for an embrace, and she returned it, the tears nearly breaking free.

Skye stepped back first, and took the seat offered to her by Giles.

"How are ye feelin', lass?"

"Fine," she lied. What else was she supposed to say? It's not like she could put into words the total devastation that consumed her. If a soul could be broken, hers certainly was.

"Must be nice to be so unaffected," James snapped.

"James Matthews." Lizzie's voice reminded her of a

mother chastising a child: stern and unyielding. Lizzie shot him a glare.

Skye looked up at James for the first time since entering the kitchen. His eyes were narrowed, his mouth pressed into a tight line.

"What?" He looked at Lizzie and then back down at the book in his hands.

"I'm sorry," Skye whispered.

"For what, exactly? Abandoning us when we needed you?" James accused, looking back up and clasping his hands in front of him on the table.

"I was only leaving because I had to."

"Please, enlighten us."

"James!" Lizzie smacked his arm.

Skye shook her head. "He has every right to be upset with me. I shouldn't have written that note, I should have called Lucas to tell him—" Her voice broke, and she covered her face with cold hands.

"Tell him what?"

Lizzie's tone was much gentler than the one she'd used on James. It almost hurt worse than James' anger. Skye didn't deserve her understanding or forgiveness.

"How come you get to push her for answers, but I can't?" James asked with no small amount of sarcasm.

"Shut up, James, or get the hell out of here. Tell him what, Skye?"

Skye swallowed hard and looked up at them. "After you guys left, I had a vision." Skye shut her eyes tightly. "I Saw my death."

Lizzie gasped. "That's never happened before! Has it?"

"No, it was a first for me and anyone in my line…as far as I know."

Giles touched her shoulder gently, pulling her gaze to his worried face. "How did ye die?"

"The Druid killed me, in front of Lucas and the rest of you."

"Oh no." Lizzie covered her mouth.

"My death is what killed you all." No need to tell them Lucas turned evil and slaughtered James before her vision had released its hold on her. "Had I not been there, the Druid wouldn't have used me, and Lucas could have won."

James didn't say a word, just sat there studying her intently.

Lizzie knelt beside her and grabbed both Skye's hands. "None of what happened is your fault, Skye."

"It *is* my fault. If I'd gone with you guys—"

"Were you planning on leaving?" James asked. "Is that why you sent us ahead?"

Skye shook her head emphatically. "No, I was going to look through the journals, that's all. It wasn't until after you left that I had the vision and realized what I needed to do."

James pushed to his feet. "Then I guess it's not *all* your fault." He disappeared out of the room.

"Don't listen to him," Lizzie told her softly. "He's grumpy and not handling it well. Apparently, being an ass is his coping mechanism."

Any other time, Skye would have laughed at the assessment. But laughter felt further away than Lucas.

"How do you not blame me? Your brother—"

"Knew what he was doing when he walked into that

building. I have to believe he will come back, that he somehow had a plan for getting out of whatever situation he found himself in."

"I'm so sorry," Skye sobbed, losing hold of the small amount of control she'd clung to.

Giles squeezed her shoulder.

Lizzie pulled her in for a hug. "I'm sorry for what you went through, I can't even imagine. If you want to talk about it, I'm here."

"I just want Lucas back."

"We'll get him back, lass." Giles' voice was soft, and Skye knew he meant every word, but it was hard for her to believe they would find a way to get to him. It wasn't like there was a map they could use. He was in the Wasteland, not fucking South Dakota.

Besides, if the Druid showed up, they were dead, and Lucas might already be dead. It was getting damn hard to find the silver lining. *And Lucas thinks I'm an optimist...*

The thought spawned a fresh wave of grief, and Skye buried her face in her hands as her shoulders silently shook.

Without any hope, how the hell was she supposed to keep going?

SKYE LOST TRACK OF TIME AS THE DAYS BLURRED together. If it hadn't been for Lizzie, she wouldn't have remembered to eat or bathe. The damp braid resting along her spine was proof that Lizzie took care of her when she couldn't—or didn't want to—take care of herself.

Currently, Skye was curled up in the armchair Lucas usually claimed. Something about being cocooned by the fabric that once surrounded him brought her a sliver of comfort. Almost as if something of him remained behind to cradle her in its memory of him.

The others murmured around her, their voices no more than the buzz of insects on a lazy summer afternoon. They took to speaking in hushed tones whenever she was present, as if their words would be the straw that finally broke her. As if anything they said could hold such power. The worst had already been done, and she hadn't fallen apart. At least not completely. She retired into herself, leaving them to carry on with their lives while she clung to the things that helped her feel close to the man she loved. A worn shirt. A pair of his boxers. His pillow. They were a sanctuary for her battered heart.

Despite her withdrawal, she hadn't completely given up. Her mind was a hive of activity even if her body was not.

Over and over her thoughts churned, as she sought an answer to the riddle that had plagued her upon waking to learn it hadn't all been a terrible nightmare. How had the Druid escaped? There was a way…she just needed to find it. Unfortunately, the only one with an answer to that question wasn't likely to share his wisdom with her.

Skye sighed and shifted in the armchair, wrapping the soft woolen blanket tighter around her body. The whisper of voices continued, the others hardly noticing she was even still sitting among them.

"You'll never figure it out, you know."

She froze, her eyes flying wide at the menacing purr she knew all too well.

No. Not here. He can't be here.

Heart pounding, Skye turned her head. A soft gasp fell from her lips when her eyes landed on the robed figure leaning against the mantelpiece.

"Not that you could do anything from here anyway, Gypsy. You don't have the power. Not to mention the fact that you couldn't even share your knowledge if you did somehow manage to stumble across a way out of the Wasteland."

Fear held her body immobile while the bandaged side of her head began to throb.

The Druid stepped away from the mantel and began to stalk toward her.

"No," Skye moaned, pressing her body back into the chair. She wouldn't survive another attack from him so soon.

"Skye?" Lizzie asked, finally pausing in her conversation with Giles and James to check on her.

The Druid held up a pale finger to his lips. "Shhh, Seer. You don't want to upset them. Only you can see me." He closed the distance easily, leaning down to whisper in her good ear, "Besides, I've missed our little chats. Haven't you?"

"No!" Skye shouted, jumping out of her chair and sending it toppling over. "You're not here! You're not here!" she cried, hands flying up to cover her head as she squeezed her eyes shut.

"Skye!" Lizzie cried.

The Druid lunged, his hands curled like he was going

to grab her, and Skye shrieked, flinging his hand away. Seeking a weapon, Skye ripped the lamp's cord out of the wall as she wrapped her fingers around its base in a death grip.

"Don't you fucking touch me," she snarled, lifting the lamp above her head, ready to smash it into his smirking face.

"Giovanni!" James shouted.

Skye blinked in confusion. Why would he call her that? Only Lucas ever called her Giovanni. Why would James want to distract her right now? Couldn't they see the danger they were in?

Lizzie's terrified whimper pulled Skye's attention back around. Lucas' sister was wide-eyed, her hands held up protectively over her head.

The arm holding the lamp started to lower as Skye scanned the room for the Druid. "Where is he? Where did he go?" she demanded, her voice bordering on hysterical.

"W-who?" Lizzie stammered.

"The Druid! He was just here."

What little color was left in Lizzie's face drained away. "Here?" she whimpered, looking around the room.

Confused, Skye finally let the lamp drop from her fingers. "Didn't you guys see him? He was right there," she said, pointing to where he'd been standing by the mantel.

"Skye, no one was here but us," James said carefully, righting the armchair.

"What?" she asked, glancing between them.

"Nay, lass. It's just us," Giles confirmed.

"But I saw him…he was talking to me…"

Giles and James exchanged a look, and Skye's cheeks burned with mortification. Great, now she was hallucinating.

"I'm sorry," she whispered, her body curling in on itself as she tried to leave the room.

"Skye, wait, you don't have to go. It's alright." Lizzie reached out to pat Skye's shoulder. "With everything you've been through, it's only natural something like this would happen. To be honest, I'd thought you were handling things entirely too well."

"Maybe for a potato," James muttered.

Lizzie glared at him. "Not funny."

James shrugged. "Doesn't make me wrong."

Skye sighed, feeling foolish. He'd looked so real, and his voice…she shuddered. That voice would haunt her for the rest of her life.

"You don't recover from something like torture overnight. PTSD is real. Look at all the soldiers out there that deal with it for years after they come back from war."

James chewed on his bottom lip thoughtfully, his eyes turning a darker shade of green as his thoughts turned inward.

"Years? Fuck me, will I never be rid of him?" Skye asked.

Lizzie frowned sympathetically. "It will just take time, sweetie. It hasn't even been a week."

Skye collapsed back into the armchair with a huff. "It feels like yesterday," she murmured, fingers caressing the edges of her bandage.

"I'm sorry I cannae do anything about the pain," Giles

said, kneeling beside her. "I know the words, but have none of the power."

Skye's eyes shot to him, a thought barreling through her mind. Digging her fingers into his arm, she practically shouted, "Wait! You used to study with the Druid, right?"

Giles flinched, but whether it was from her volume or the pressure of her nails into his skin, Skye didn't know.

"I did," he agreed, trying to pry her fingers off of him.

Skye dropped his arm. "What do you know about getting to the Wasteland? You helped Maggie send Oliver there. You must remember something."

"Skye, what are you asking?" Lizzie asked, perching on the edge of the couch beside the Scot.

Excitement bubbled within her as the idea continued to grow and take shape. "We know how to send someone to the Wasteland, assuming Giles remembers. If that's the case, it can't be a far stretch that we can figure out how to bring someone back. I mean…these kinds of things usually have a counter or some type of reversal, right?"

Giles shook his head, his green eyes apologetic. "Lass, that's not how it works. The ritual is a one-way ticket."

Despair clawed at her. "No," Skye insisted, unwilling to lose the only piece of hope she'd had in days. "There has to be a way."

James rested a hand on Lizzie's shoulder. "You said that you thought Maggie might still be alive in the Wasteland," he reminded the older man.

Skye shot him a grateful look, thankful that someone else was on her side.

Giles' eyes narrowed. "I said I thought her body had

made its way to the Wasteland, not that she was alive. I watched her die."

"But her body was still sent there, or so you believe. Doesn't that mean there's a way to send a non-Druid?"

"Only if the person is dead!" he cried. "I don't exactly see how that will be helpful!"

"What if only one of them is dead?" Lizzie asked thoughtfully.

The other three turned to stare at her.

"What do you mean?" James asked.

"Well, my gran sacrificed herself to complete the ritual, but who's to say that if someone had been touching her body once the ritual was completed, they wouldn't have made the jump with her?"

"You're forgetting that the Druid was also sent. That's already two bodies that made the jump if you include him."

Lizzie's eyes flared with excitement. "So, all we need to do is re-enact the ritual, and we can find Lucas."

"Yeah, if one of us dies in the process," James pointed out, his brows low.

"I'll do it," Giles said quickly, his face still leeched of color but pinched with determination.

Skye's mouth fell open in surprise. "But why?"

His eyes darkened before closing. Letting out a sigh, Giles whispered, "Because it's my fault this happened in the first place. It's the least I can do to set things right. If you really believe that there's a possibility this could work, Seer. Then I will offer my life, gladly."

The room filled with stunned silence.

"Giles," Lizzie murmured, "no one expects you to do this."

"I know, lass. But I offer all the same."

"This is all still hypothetical anyway," James pointed out. "Assuming it works, and we send someone over there, how the hell are they supposed to bring Lucas *back*?"

As suddenly as it blossomed, Skye's hope flickered and died. Getting to Lucas was only half the battle. Giles' sacrifice would mean nothing if it didn't result in Lucas returning home.

Skye slumped back in her chair. "So much for that idea."

"It was hardly a solid one," James said. "More like half a plan at best."

Skye glared at him.

James held up a hand. "I'm just saying it wasn't a plan, not by itself. But it was a start. We can build on it."

"Yeah, if we can find out how to bring Lucas home. The only person who ever escaped the Wasteland was the Druid. You think he's going to just hand that secret over? Assuming we can even find him?"

"What if we don't give him a choice?" Lizzie asked, her eyes distant.

"How are we supposed to manage that? We don't even have Lucas' power to rely on."

"No," Lizzie agreed, her voice thoughtful. "But we have yours."

Skye's brows scrunched together in confusion. "How are visions of the dead helpful?"

"We pretend," James said, grinning as he squeezed Lizzie's shoulder. "Lizzie, that's a brilliant idea."

"I'm not following..."

"You tell the Druid you had another vision. We'll use it to convince him to tell us how he escaped."

"Guys...the odds of him falling for that..." She looked around, wondering if they were all seriously considering this. Even Giles looked convinced. "You know the only thing this asshole holds sacred is his power. He's not going to do anything to risk it."

"Not unless not acting would be a greater risk to it," Giles said.

Skye clasped her hands in her lap. Had everyone lost their damn minds? Not even thirty minutes ago she was hearing voices, and now, these three were talking about willingly seeking out the man that wanted them all dead. To ask for help.

"There's no fucking way," Skye said.

"Hear me out," Lizzie said over her protest.

Skye folded her arms across her chest and looked at her expectantly.

"What if you tell him you saw him die, because the power was too much for him on his own? That he needs Lucas here, alive, to help him maintain enough control. That should be enough to pique his interest."

"And he's supposed to what, just bring Lucas back?"

"Well," James started, "maybe you tell him you might know a way to get to him, all you need is to know how he got out so you can bring him back."

"That's a hell of an assumption. He'll likely kill me on the spot," Skye said with a snort.

James shrugged. "I think we're on to something."

"You guys are fucking crazy."

"I might be able to help you convince him," Giles interjected.

"How?" Skye asked dubiously.

"I'll go instead. Ye're right, he'd be skeptical of ye seeking him out willingly. But I could tell him of the vision. He might still believe me, and he knows that I know the spell to get to the Wasteland. We were friends, once. He has less reason to mistrust me."

"Do you really think that will work?" Lizzie asked, leaning forward.

Giles shrugged.

"Not a chance," Skye muttered with a shake of her head. "Have you all forgotten who we're dealing with?"

"No one's forgotten, Skye. But you aren't the only one who's lost someone here. We are all hurting, and we all want him back. We've got to at least try."

Lizzie's earnest gaze hurt to look at, so Skye stared at the wall. Those bright blue eyes were entirely too like her brother's.

Skye finally sighed. "The fucker's going to kill us all anyway. I guess there's no harm in expediting the process," she said. "If we're going to convince him, he's going to need to hear it from me." Although, the thought of having to face him had Skye digging her fingers into the arms of her chair to keep her from fleeing from the room.

"That's the spirit," James said.

A snicker left her lips before she consciously realized it. She blinked in surprise as the others' shoulders started to shake with laughter. Even Giles thought it was funny, although it was hard to tell with his lips pressed together.

Fighting a smile, Skye rolled her eyes. "Fuck it, let's do it. How do you propose we find him?"

"I might be able to help with that, too," Giles said, adjusting his glasses.

Skye waved her hand, gesturing for him to continue. "The floor is yours."

The others leaned in close as Giles started to explain his plan.

CHAPTER 15

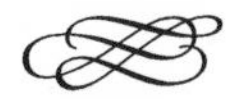

LUCAS

Death. It was the main thing on Lucas' mind these days. At least, he thought it had been days. Or was it months by now? He had no fucking clue anymore.

He laid on the hot sand, surrounded by nothing but more fucking sand. Surely death would be preferable to this hellhole.

Lucas opened his eyes and looked up into the colorless sky. The sun should have beat down on him with its rays of yellow, red, and orange, but instead, it was completely void of color, just like the rest of this world.

"Lucas."

He closed his eyes. *Not now, please not now.*

"Lucas, are you dead?"

"Unfortunately not." He opened his eyes and pushed to his feet, unable to resist the siren-like allure of her.

She stood about five feet away, looking just as beautiful as she had the first time he'd ever laid his miserable eyes on her.

"What's it going to be this time, Skye?" Lucas spat out her name, knowing the woman standing before him was not the one who held his heart. "Here to torment me some more?"

Unfortunately, for all that his mind knew the difference, his body did not. The fact that she was also the only company he had in this shithole made her absolutely irresistible—even if their interactions always left him feeling ripped to shreds by the time she was done with him.

She laughed, a bright cheerful sound that was entirely out of place here. "Of course not, silly. I'm just here to keep you company."

"By reminding me of my failures."

Wasteland Skye shrugged. "There wouldn't be anything to remind you of if you'd kept me safe as you promised."

His heart pinched, and he clenched his jaw. Lucas began walking, desperate to put as much distance between them as possible. She was easier to ignore if he wasn't looking at her. Not that she'd let him go far. She never did; she'd just tag along, tormenting him until his mind broke.

Wasteland Skye was his demon, the most painful manifestation of his failures. Eventually, the weight of those mistakes would drown him.

Maybe I can walk myself to death. The thought of death, by any means, was just more wishful thinking. He'd already tried. If death were possible here, the endless days with nothing to eat or drink would've taken him by now.

"Don't want to talk?" she asked, catching up to him. "That's fine with me."

"Don't you have anything else to do? Someone else to toy with? I can't be the only miserable bastard trapped here."

"If you didn't believe you deserved it, you'd never have created me. You're my sole responsibility."

"Fucking awesome."

Just ahead, the ground sloped upward, and Lucas dug his feet into the sand as he climbed the hill.

"Maybe you should stop."

"Maybe you should fuck off."

"I'm serious, Lucas."

"So am I."

"Detective Loomis!"

He spun, beyond enraged at her use of the real Skye's nickname for him. It broke something in him, to hear those words while he was trapped here.

"You have no fucking right!" he yelled. "You are not her! You are not real!"

"Who are you trying to convince, Detective? You or me?" she asked with a flirtatious smile. "You know I'm as real as she is. Don't believe me? Feel for yourself..." She took a step toward him, the seductive roll of her hips all too familiar. Revulsion and lust spiraled inside of him. There was nothing he wanted more than to pull Skye into his arms and bury himself in her body, but this demon was the furthest thing from the woman he loved. The hard glint in her amber eyes was proof enough of that. Skye would never be that calculating.

Lucas ground his teeth together. "Not interested."

This was her M.O....she'd push him with insults, throw

his mistakes in his face, then try to seduce him. It had almost worked.

Once.

Never again. Lucas shut his eyes tightly, remembering the images that flooded his mind the second the evil bitch had touched her lips to his.

Images of his Skye, beaten and bloody.

"Oh, come on, Lucas, what's it going to cost you? Nothing. You're already here and obviously not going anywhere. It's just you and me forever, baby. Isn't that what you want?"

She ran her fingers along the exposed skin of his arm. Her touch seared him, and Lucas jolted away.

"He got out," Lucas reminded her, stepping back to move out of her reach.

"True," she murmured coyly, pulling her dark braid over her shoulder to play with the ends.

Lucas forgot to breathe as he stared, transfixed as her nimble fingers wove in and out of the satiny strands. Memories of all the times he'd watched her do the exact thing tumbled over themselves in his mind.

"He's *lifetimes* more powerful than you, though. Something you seem to keep forgetting."

Lucas' lungs burned as air finally found its way back into his body, her words setting him free. Angry she'd slipped under his guard, Lucas' voice dropped to a guttural growl. "No, he's not. We share the same amount of power, remember? Besides, that asshole may have gotten the jump on me, but Skye and the others got out. That means, power or not, he can be outsmarted. And, once I learn how to use my power, he'll be no match for me."

"Once you learn? Planning on going somewhere?" She snickered. "Good luck with that."

Lucas bit back a retort, annoyed with himself for picking a fight with what was essentially a figment of his imagination.

"Are you sure they escaped?"

Lucas glared at her. "Yes, I am."

"You're wrong," she sneered. "He cut them down where they stood. Slaughtered Lizzie and Matthews, then took me as his own."

"You're lying!" Lucas shouted, his face and ears burning. Inside, his power roared, eager to be set free.

Wasteland Skye laughed again, the chilling sound nothing like his Skye. "You're so easy, you know that?"

Lucas spun away, fighting the urge to let his power slam into that small body. He'd made that mistake before, too. And when she'd stared up at him with wet eyes and blood dripping from her mouth, Lucas had fallen on his knees and sobbed beside her. It was pure agony to see the result of what the Druid had done to her, but it was absolutely soul crushing to see her in the same state because of something he'd done himself—whether it was real or just some fucked-up illusion.

Lucas wouldn't survive the experience again. Not without losing the final pieces of his sanity.

He started walking again, his heart pounding as he tried to push away the coil of emotions at war within him. The wind gusted, sending sand flying all around. Lucas shielded his eyes and moved faster, nearly running down the hill. If he could get to the base, he might be somewhat protected from the incoming sandstorm.

This fucking place couldn't give him so much as a peaceful breeze, but it sure as hell loved throwing sand in his eyes—and down his throat—from time to time.

"This is going to be fun," Wasteland Skye said with a giggle. "Better shield yourself, Detective. We can't have that pretty face of yours getting scarred."

"Fuck you."

He ran faster, and tripped, his body rolling down to the base of the hill. The sand cut at his skin and stuck to him where hot blood welled. He groaned, the pain ten times worse than it ought to be for such minor injuries. The sand cut like glass and burned like poison where it ground into his wounds.

"Well, that was attractive."

Ignoring her and the pain, Lucas stood, bracing himself against the wind. As he moved along the base of the dune, trying to use it for cover, he noticed a dark spot that didn't quite fit in with the rest of the place.

"What the hell is that?"

Peering out against the storm, Lucas pushed through the wind toward what appeared to be a cavern.

In the middle of nowhere.

"Definitely go inspect a dark cave! That's an awesome idea, Lucas," his tormentor shouted behind him sarcastically. "You do always have the best plans, don't you?"

The wind whipped around him, nearly throwing him back twice before he reached the inside of the cavern. It was dark, but protected from the storm raging just outside its entrance. He walked farther inside and sat against the wall to wait out the storm. It wasn't much, but it was better than nothing.

"So, we're just going to sit here, then?" Skye teased, moving to sit beside him.

If she touched him, he'd snap. Lucas shut his eyes and clenched his jaw, trying to ignore the tantalizing scent of her.

"Please go away."

Seeing her, even the fake her, was taking its toll. Truth was, he couldn't figure out why he hadn't gone full *Shining* already. He still *felt* normal, and other than seeing Wasteland Skye, he wasn't hallucinating.

Not like you'd know if you were going insane, dumbass.

When she didn't answer, Lucas opened his eyes and breathed a sigh of relief. She was gone. *Finally.* Not that she'd stay gone. She always came back. She probably wouldn't stay away until she'd claimed the last pieces of his fucking soul.

Maybe he should just give in; it wasn't like a soul was going to do him any good while trapped here.

The wind screamed outside, and the storm grew so strong it completely blacked out any light, casting him in complete darkness.

Perfect.

Just as quickly as it came, the storm died, and a dim light returned to the cavern. Without knowing how much time he had, Lucas pushed to his feet. *Might as well explore…*

He brushed sand from his hair and clothes, then turned to survey the small space he'd found.

"What the hell?"

Light from the mouth of the cave cast a light onto the

back wall he'd been leaning against. Someone had painted dark runes all over the space, though Lucas didn't recognize the meaning of them. The swirls and lines were similar enough to the spells he'd been practicing back home, but these felt…dead to him. Void of all magic, despite the fact that they'd had to be painted by someone who knew what they were doing.

Someone like my bastard grandfather.

Moving closer, it soon became obvious that they'd been painted in blood. Of course, they had. Fucking Druids and their penchant for bleeding all over the place.

Did I just find his hideout?

Maybe there would be a clue about how he managed to escape…Lucas took a tentative step forward, not trusting his luck. Everything about this place had been a trap meant to ensnare his mind and break his will. What would make this cave any different?

His foot kicked a rock, sending it clattering across the stone floor. Leaning down, he lifted it. Someone had sharpened the edge, turning it into a blade.

A blade that was covered in dried blood.

Investigating the space as if it was one of his crime scenes, Lucas found more of the swirling symbols, as well as what appeared to be tally marks carved into the hard stone. By the looks of it, whoever made the runes had been trapped here for decades, more evidence this was the Druid's cave. *Or, maybe that's just what he wants you to think,* a cautious voice warned. Lucas ignored it, focusing instead on the hope blooming in his chest.

For the first time since Lucas woke up in the Wasteland, a smile spread across his face.

This had to be it! Somewhere in these bloody symbols was the way out of this godforsaken place.

Now, he just needed to find it.

CHAPTER 16

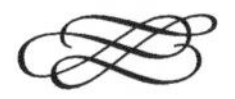

LIZZIE

Soft firelight danced around the room, casting a romantic glow in the bedroom. The crackling of the wood as it burned should have soothed her, but Lizzie was far from calm. No matter how many times or various ways she distracted herself, eventually the worries would worm their way back into the forefront of her mind.

James' fingers traced soft circles against her palm as they both stared up at the ceiling in silence. Stolen moments like this were few and far between these days. Dealing with Skye was almost like adopting a puppy—actually, it was more like adopting ten puppies—and Lizzie was on constant Skye patrol in an attempt to mitigate the damage she was doing to her body by refusing to take care of herself. Lizzie wished it was as easy to prevent the damage to her heart.

Skye had lost all interest in caring for herself. Basic hygiene was a thing of the past, and food usually sat untouched until Lizzie threatened to force feed her. Somedays, it was worse than dealing with a two-year-old.

Scratch that. A two-year-old would be easier, at least they would tell you what they wanted. Skye barely formed words most days. Unless she was muttering to herself. Most of the time, she was practically catatonic, and Lizzie wasn't sure that was the less frightening of the two states. If they didn't find a way to reach Lucas soon, Lizzie didn't think there was anything that would keep the Skye she knew from fading away completely.

Lizzie closed her eyes, and a tear slipped down her cheek. Her brother was out there somewhere, stranded in the Wasteland, and they were no closer to finding him.

"Hey," James said softly, wiping the tear away. "What is it?"

Lizzie opened her eyes but didn't look at him. "What if we never find him?" Her voice was barely above a whisper, as if she could keep the words from being true if no one else heard them.

"Lucas?"

The absurdity of his need to ask sparked the hint of temper never far from the surface. "No, the Prince of England. Who else would I be talking about?"

James leaned back against the pillow and propped his head up on an arm. His hazel eyes were filled with understanding. "We'll find him."

"How do you know that? We've been trying for over a week, and we're no closer than we were the night he was sent there. What if this is it? What if we have to spend the rest of our lives without him? Are we just hiding here, avoiding the inevitable?"

"And just what is the inevitable, Lizzie?"

She bit her lip and stared up at the ceiling, as shadows

danced on the plaster until tears blurred her vision. "Our deaths."

James sat up fully, the sheet dropping to his hips. "You think the Druid killing us is inevitable?"

Lizzie moved to face him, and his eyes dropped to her chest. With a sigh, she tugged the sheet up to cover her bare breasts. James pouted, but lifted his eyes back to her face.

"Without Lucas, what else is going to happen? I'm not magical, you aren't a Druid, and other than being able to see what might happen, Skye has no real power. Hell, Skye is barely functioning right now. We're screwed if he comes after us, James."

James brushed a finger down her cheek. "Since when are you so quick to give up?"

"I just know when to admit I've lost."

"We haven't lost."

"It sure feels like it," she muttered, looking away.

Tilting her chin up until her eyes met his, James insisted, "Lucas is alive, Lizzie, not dead. That means we still have a shot. You think your brother would have given up and accepted you were dead if the roles were reversed?"

The words were like a blow to her gut. Gaping, Lizzie stared at him, hurt and anger making it hard to speak. "You think I want him to be dead?"

"I think you and Skye both want it to be over, one way or another."

"I don't want any of this," Lizzie said softly, more tears spilling down her cheeks. "I want my brother back, but I also don't want to have false hope. I'm a realist."

James let out a breath. "You would never have said shit like that before."

"Excuse me?"

"Before Jeff."

Lizzie sucked in a breath. "What the hell does that asshole have to do with anything?"

"You were always an optimist—frustratingly so—until he got to you. Ever since then, I've watched you steadily morphing into a pessimist."

"First of all, you didn't know me before I met him, and secondly, what is the bright side of our current situation, James? Please enlighten me."

"Just because we didn't speak much before your marriage doesn't mean I didn't know you, Liz. Fuck, I've been half in love with you since the day you bounced into the precinct to bring Lucas some of your homemade muffins. Which, in case you don't remember, was the day Lucas and I got partnered up."

She wasn't sure what to say. She'd been so wrapped up in the newness of her relationship with Jeff she'd barely noticed the dark-haired detective working with her brother.

James sat forward and linked his fingers with hers, his voice gentle but insistent. "The bright side here, baby, is that your brother is alive. If I know him as well as I think I do, he's probably already searching for a way back so he can kick ass and take names."

Lizzie chuckled. She could almost picture Lucas, red-faced and beating his fists against a wall trying to make his own door home.

"If you think, for one second, that I'm okay with rolling over and giving up, you don't know me at all,

Lizzie MacConnell. I have every intention of having a future with you. One that involves Greece, you in a white dress walking down an aisle, and, hopefully, kids."

Lizzie smiled despite the lump in her throat. She wanted all those things, too, but how long were they supposed to hold on to hope? How long was she expected to wear this mask like she wasn't slowly dying inside?

"I love you, Liz."

"I love you, too."

James cupped her face and pulled her body against his. His lips were soft on hers, and she pressed against him, wanting more. He trailed his fingers down her bare back, and Lizzie shivered from the touch.

A scream ripped through the relative quiet of the cottage, and they pulled apart as if they'd been scorched by flames.

"What the hell was that?"

"Skye!" Lizzie answered, already out of bed and pulling on a robe.

Ripping the door open, she ran down the hall toward the sobbing. Another scream sounded, and James pulled her back, stepping in front of her.

"Let me go in first."

Lizzie nodded, and he rounded the corner into the living room. Curiosity overriding concern for herself, Lizzie followed a few seconds later. Giles stood in the center of the room staring at a cowering Skye.

"Stay away from me!" she screamed, her eyes red and swollen from crying.

"What happened?" James demanded.

The older man's hands trembled as he ran them

through his hair. Wide-eyed, he shook his head. "I haven't a bloody clue. We were sittin' on the couch, readin' through her Gran's journals, when she grew panicked and pale. I tried to speak to the lass, but she started shriekin' and throwin' whatever she could reach at me, includin' her fists when she ran out of options."

Lizzie studied Giles. His lip was bleeding from the corner, but he was otherwise unharmed. "She hit you?"

He nodded. "Got me bloody good, too." He touched his split lip with a wince. "Haven't been hit that hard since the last pub fight I got myself into."

"Skye," James said, his voice low as he knelt in front of her.

She didn't look at him, but stared through him. "No, no, no," she chanted. "What more do you want from me? You've already taken everything!"

Lizzie hugged herself, worrying at her lower lip. Her earlier thoughts of slowly dying inside popping into her mind. She'd had it all wrong; she wasn't the one dying, Skye was. Bit by bit, every day, she was losing more of herself to the memory of what that bastard had done to her. The stubborn, sassy woman who'd become such an important part of their lives was shattering, and there was only one person who could help her pick up the pieces.

Unfortunately for them, they had to find him first.

"Skye." Lizzie crossed the room and knelt beside James.

Skye cringed and pressed back into the wall, squeezing her eyes shut. Tears splashed down her cheeks and snot dripped from her nose, but she didn't bother wiping her face. "Please stop," she begged, her voice heartbreakingly child-like.

"Skye, the Druid isn't here."

Shaking, she raised her hands, pressing them against the sides of her head, as if trying to drown out whatever her imaginary Druid was saying.

James called her name, but she didn't so much as flinch. She was lost to whatever horror show was playing out in front of her. Trying again, he gently grasped her wrist and pulled it away from her good ear. "Skye, you're safe. We've got you, and we won't let him get you again."

Wanting to do something, Lizzie reached forward and touched Skye's leg. Skye flinched and pulled it back into her body. Dropping her arms to her knees, she began to rock like a frightened child.

"Skye, open your eyes," Lizzie pleaded.

Skye's eyelids fluttered open, and for the first time, she looked directly at Lizzie. Swallowing, she rasped, "Lizzie?"

Lizzie nodded, her heart breaking all over at the pain reflected in her friend's eyes. Skye slumped forward, and Lizzie wrapped her arms around her as her shoulders shook.

"I don't know what to do," she cried. "He won't leave me alone."

"Shhhhhhh, it's okay." Lizzie rubbed her hand over Skye's tangled mess of hair. "He won't get you again, I promise."

James ran a hand down Lizzie's back and gave her an encouraging smile before getting to his feet. "Let's get a drink, Giles."

"A dram of scotch would be much appreciated."

The two men left the room while Lizzie held onto Skye. Pressing her cheek against the other woman's head, Lizzie cradled her and promised, "We will find Lucas, Skye. And then we'll send that bastard Druid straight to hell."

CHAPTER 17

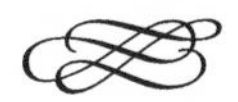

SKYE

Shame burned in her cheeks, and she scooted deeper into her cave of blankets. *I am losing my mind.* She'd been so damn sure he was really there this time.

His voice echoed in her head, and Skye shivered, nervously peeking over the top of her blanket to ensure she was still alone in Lucas' bed.

One ragged breath.

Two.

Relaxing only slightly, she closed her eyes.

There was no rational explanation for her hallucinations, or her reaction to them. Whatever the Druid had done to her while she'd been chained in that warehouse had left its imprint on her soul. She might have gotten away from him physically, but it was growing increasingly clear she'd never escape him fully.

Some wounds never truly healed.

Skye could barely stand to be in her own company right now; she was a complete fucking mess. Hiding under the blankets and imagining the boogie man waiting for her beneath the bed… or in a shadowed corner of the room—this wasn't her. She was stronger than this. With only herself to count on for so long, Skye learned how to be tough. Or at least, she had been, once upon a time.

She could find no hint of the woman she used to be in the haunted eyes that stared back at her from the mirror each morning. Some crucial element of her was missing now. The Druid had stolen it from her when he carved his first rune into her flesh. Or maybe she lost it when he beat her night after night only to patch her together and start over again. Or when he tore off her ear like it was some sinister souvenir…and that wasn't even considering what the loss of Lucas was doing to her.

Nothing felt safe anymore. Not even her mind could be her sanctuary now, so filled with ghosts as it was.

Skye was tainted. Tainted by the Druid's magic. Tainted by his touch.

Revulsion crawled over her skin like a thousand disgusting insects. There was no escape when your prison was in your mind.

Blinking back tears, Skye forced herself to stay present and not get lost in another crushing wave of grief.

"If someone's listening…I-I need your help. Please…if you could just send me a sign…I'm" —she choked back a sob— "I'm not sure how much longer I can fight this without knowing there's a light at the end of the tunnel."

Skye didn't know what she was asking for, or even who she asked, only that she was on the brink of going under, and this time, she wasn't sure she'd resurface.

Rolling over onto her side, she brought her knees up to

her chest and did the only thing she could: she breathed… and eventually, she fell asleep.

"Skye, honey, you really need to take better care of yourself."

"Gran? What are you doing in my studio?" Skye looked away from the red and purple swirls on her canvas and over to the bespectacled woman hovering just inside of the door.

"Just stopping by for a visit."

"Now?" Skye glanced at her wrist, trying to gauge the time, but the hands of her watch were frozen, and the symbols looked like...music notes? She blinked, trying to make sense of what she was seeing, but the numbers never came into focus. Definitely a good time for a break.

"Is there ever a bad time to visit my favorite granddaughter?"

Skye rolled her eyes. "Gran, I'm your only *granddaughter."*

"So?" she challenged with a lift of her silvery brow.

Knowing it was a losing argument, Skye laughed and held her arms open for a hug.

"That's more like it," Janice murmured, stepping into Skye's arms and squeezing tight.

The scent of roses and honeysuckle filled her nose, and loss more potent than anything she'd ever felt crashed into her. Skye fought against unexpected tears. She took a step back from her Gran, blinking in confusion. What in the world was wrong with her? Why would a hug make her feel so…alone?

Placing a hand on either side of her cheeks, her Gran studied her with eyes that saw everything. The deep chocolate and gold-flecked orbs were filled with pity. "I'm so sorry, sweetheart."

"Sorry? What are you talking about?"

"If there was more time, I would pretend with you for a while longer, but I'm not supposed to be here as it is. I don't think they'll let that go unnoticed."

"Pretend? They? Gran, are you feeling okay?"

Janice bat away Skye's hand as she tried to take her temperature. "I'm fine, Skylar. I need you to listen to me."

Skye froze, her back going ramrod straight. Her Gran only ever called her by her full name when she was in trouble. Slowly taking a seat in a chair draped with a paint-splattered cloth, Skye looked up at her Gran. "I'm listening."

"I know you've read the journals."

Guilt gnawed at her, and Skye started to squirm. "Gran, I—"

"No need to apologize, honey. I wouldn't have left them for you if you weren't meant to read them. What's important now is that you take the lessons with you."

"Lessons?"

"Tine minte amria."

Tingles raced up and down Skye's limbs, and her ears filled with the beating of her racing heart. Why did she recognize those words?

"The curse is breaking, Skye, but it's not yet broken. In order for you both to be free, you must—" Janice broke off

with a frown and glanced over her shoulder. With a curse, she turned back to Skye. "I'm out of time. Skye, everything you need, you already have. The answer is there. Look within yourself to find it. Remember what you've Seen. Remember..."

~

SKYE SAT UP WITH A GASP, THE FRANTIC BEAT OF HER heart the only sound in the room. With shaking hands, she wiped her wet cheeks, wonder and surprise momentarily pushing out the heartache.

She hadn't dreamed of her grandmother since, well, since the night after her funeral. Skye remembered that dream vividly because when it happened, she'd thought it was real. Then, like tonight, Janice had visited Skye while she was working in her studio, just to ask about her day and tell her how proud of her she was. Skye remembered thinking it was a gift, that her Gran's spirit had returned to let Skye know that she was all right and not to worry.

This time, she *knew* it was a gift. Skye had asked the universe to send her a sign, and Janice Giovanni had answered.

Even though she wasn't sure what exactly the answer meant, for the first time, she wasn't afraid of failing. If her Gran told her she had what she needed, Skye believed her.

"Thank you," Skye whispered, pressing her fingers to her lips.

The pain was still there, along with the grief, but this time, when Skye snuggled back into the blankets, there was also the smallest flicker of hope.

~

For the first time in over a week, Skye woke before Lizzie's falsely cheerful knock on the door. Pushing her feet over the side of the bed, she grabbed what she needed and headed for the shower.

A grim sort of determination fueled her motions, helping her focus only on the task directly in front of her. She listed the tasks off in her head as she picked up the necessary items. Shampoo. *Check.* Conditioner. *Check.* Razor. *Dear God, when was the last time I shaved?*

Less than an hour later, with a fresh bandage in place, a towel carefully wrapped around her head, and toothpaste foaming out of her mouth, Skye felt like a new person. Maybe not quite who she'd been before, but certainly more human than zombie. *I wonder how long it will last.*

With a grimace, she rinsed her mouth out with water and began to work at the tangled knots in her hair. A particularly snared piece brought tears to her eyes. *That's what happens when you don't wash your hair for a week, genius.*

The sun had barely risen when she padded down the hall, dressed and ready to face the day. Well, maybe not the day, but at least a steaming cup of coffee. It was something.

The voices reached her before she made it to the living room.

"I don't know what to do with her anymore," Lizzie said, her voice pitched low. "This morning she didn't even bother to growl at me when I knocked."

"Maybe we need to talk about a plan that doesn't hinge

on her having to face her captor. She's certainly not in the right mental or emotional state," James replied, just as quietly.

Heart pounding, Skye pressed against the wall, their words beating at the fragile armor she'd wrapped herself in.

"Can you blame her?" Lizzie snapped before sighing. "Maybe you're right. We can't ask her to do that. You saw what happened last night when she just thought he was near her. I can't imagine what will happen if she actually has to come face to face with him."

This is your chance, Giovanni. Do you hear what they think of you? You either go in there right now and prove them wrong, or you stay hidden over here and prove that you're too weak to pull your weight. Too weak to help save Lucas.

Just as she was straightening, her doubt took center stage in her mind. *What if they're right? Sometimes the heart is willing, but the body is incapable. Do you really think you can walk away from him unscathed?*

Fingering the fresh bandages at what used to be her ear, Skye turned the question over in her mind. *Yes.* Maybe not unscathed, but she could do this. She *had* to do this. Not just for Lucas, which would have been enough on its own, but for herself. It was the only way to regain what that asshole had taken from her.

Taking the last step that brought her into the weak light of the living room, Skye said, "I know that I haven't been the most reliable ally recently, and I understand why you hesitate to trust me, but I can do this."

Lizzie's cheeks turned a mottled red, and her eyes widened.

Before she could apologize, Skye held up her hands. "No, it's okay. You guys are right. What he did to me…the things that are replaying on a loop in my mind, they're ugly. But I am tired of letting him hold that power over me. I don't want to be the girl that jumps at her own shadow, and there might be days now where I can't help but turn into her, but when it's my choice, *if* it's my choice, I choose not to be that girl. Please give me the chance to prove it."

Lizzie was crying freely by the time she'd finished speaking, and even James had to look away to hide whatever her admission had done to him. It was the first time she'd really expressed how much effort it took simply to get out of bed. They had witnessed it, but they hadn't understood it, not really. Now, maybe, they were at least starting to.

Throwing her arms around her, Lizzie said, "Of course, whatever you need. But only if you're sure, Skye. We don't want to make you do anything you aren't ready to do."

"I'm ready," she assured her with a smile that felt entirely too foreign.

Arms tightening around her again, Lizzie whispered, "I've missed you."

Swallowing, Skye closed her eyes, pushing away the tears that threatened to fall. *No more crying.* "I've missed me, too."

"What changed?" Lizzie asked, stepping back from her.

Skye blushed, knowing that the question wasn't meant to be a jab.

With an apologetic smile, Lizzie handed her an untouched cup of coffee. "I'm sorry, I didn't mean it that way, but when you went to bed last night…"

Sipping at the still warm coffee, Skye didn't need her to finish the explanation. She remembered all too clearly the state she'd been in last night, the state she'd been in more often than not since they brought her home. Hating the reminder, Skye set the cup down on the coffee table and said simply, "I had a dream."

James gave a startled laugh. "A dream?"

She threw him a half-smile. "Gran visited me."

Sitting up straighter, he eyed her with what she'd come to recognize as his detective eyes. The look reminded her entirely too much of Lucas, and she had to look away to catch her breath.

Lizzie brushed warm fingers over the back of her hand. "Like a dream-dream, or a *Dream*?"

Skye shrugged. "I'm not sure, but Gran has only visited me in my sleep once before. So, I would like to assume it was more than just my subconscious."

Nodding sympathetically, Lizzie asked, "What did she say?"

Running her fingers along the wet ends of her braid, Skye took a seat beside Lizzie on the couch. "That I have everything I need. That the curse is breaking but not broken. To remember what I've Seen."

"Couldn't be more specific, huh?" James said with a grin.

Skye let out a little laugh.

"Any idea what she was referring to?"

"Not yet," Skye admitted with a shake of her head. "But it can't be too hard to figure out. Most of my visions lately have been about Lucas and the Druid facing off, but those have all changed now because he sent Lucas to the Wasteland. So, it has to be something I Saw during those other visions."

James nodded. "I tend to agree with your assumption."

"I've been jotting down the details of the visions, just in case they ended up being relevant. So, I was planning on looking through my notebook to see if anything jumped out at me."

"Like your Gran's journals," Lizzie said.

Skye smiled her first truly genuine smile. "Exactly."

"Good idea," Lizzie murmured.

"In the meantime, we should probably call Giles and tell him we're ready to put his idea into action," James said as he stood.

Skye nodded. "One way or the other, it's time to stop hiding."

CHAPTER 18

SKYE

Eyeing Giles' swollen lip, Skye fought the impulse to run and hide. "I'm so sorry," she moaned, mortification burning her cheeks.

"'Tis okay, lass. I probably deserved it for one thing or another." He winked.

Feeling too guilty to accept his forgiveness, Skye shook her head. "No, you don't. Whatever else you've done, all you've tried to do since we got here is help us."

He placed gentle hands on each of her shoulders. "I know it was an accident. I've seen that look in grown men's eyes before. Facing a demon is never pretty. Especially when it's got its sharp claws in ye."

All she could do was nod, grateful to hear that he truly did understand. Then again, between being friends with the Druid before he'd gone postal and watching his other friend sacrifice her own life, it was likely Giles had battled plenty of his own demons.

"Right, now that we've got that out of the way. Ye said

ye were ready to give the spell a try." He looked over her shoulder at Lizzie.

"Yes," Lizzie agreed.

James frowned as he watched Lizzie. Worry was evident in the creases around his eyes and lips. He wasn't stoked on the idea of her placing herself in danger, but there was no other choice. Lizzie knew the risks, and they'd all agreed that her brother was worth every one of them.

"Do you really think it will work?" Lizzie asked, following Giles into the living room.

Giles shrugged. "It's a minor spell, no rune work required. Since ye are part of the O'Leary-MacConnell bloodline, I do not see why it shouldn't."

"Except for the part where I'm female and don't have any claim to a Druid's actual power," Lizzie pointed out.

"Maybe not the raw power, no, but that doesn't mean there isn't a trace of magic in ye."

"Anyone who's tasted her coffee already knows it's a magic elixir," Skye muttered.

James and Lizzie laughed.

"Can't argue with that," James said.

Turning back to Giles, Lizzie asked, "So, how does this work?"

"We will start by cleansing the room."

Lizzie glanced around the pristine room. "It looks pretty clean to me."

"Cleanse, not clean," he clarified, holding out a thick bundle of sage.

Lizzie mouthed a silent 'oh.'

"Isn't that what people do when they think a place is haunted?" James asked, wrinkling his nose.

Skye couldn't quite contain her laughter. "It's to help cleanse a space of negative energy."

He eyed the sage dubiously. "If you say so."

Nodding, Giles continued, "Then we will cast a circle—"

"Like witches do in the movies?" Lizzie blurted.

Giles chuckled. "Exactly."

"What does that do?"

"It's for protection," Skye answered for him, familiar with the practice.

"Once we've prepared the space, then we can begin the evocation."

"The what?"

"Evocation, a calling of the spirit, or in this case, a particular spirit. If it works, the Druid will feel drawn to this place. With his power, he can send his spirit here to investigate, while his body remains wherever he is actually located, lowering the risk to us."

"What if his body decides it doesn't want to remain behind?" James asked, his voice hard as his hand moved to his hip where his gun was usually holstered.

"He is too curious by nature to take the time to travel by natural means, and with the protection spells Lucas put in place before he left, Oliver can no longer portal here directly."

Lizzie shuddered at the use of her grandfather's name. They'd made a point to refer to him only as 'the Druid' since he was far from the man she and Lucas remembered as Pop.

"I thought you said that Lucas' interfering with the Druid's original runes was a problem," James asked with a frown.

"I said that it would let Oliver know ye were here, but he already knows that now, so there's no point in pretending otherwise. He could find us here anytime he wanted. What he won't be anticipating is *us* seeking *him* out."

"He thinks he won," Skye said darkly.

Giles nodded, his eyes hidden behind the glare bouncing off his glasses. It gave him a supernatural look that had goose-bumps erupting down her arms. Skye blinked, and the illusion broke as he turned away from her and back toward the others.

"All ye have to do is repeat after me and focus all of yer intent and energy on the words as ye speak them. It would probably help if ye could also picture him as ye do."

Lizzie paled, and Skye didn't blame her. Even the thought of the Druid's spirit appearing before them was enough to make her nauseous.

"Do ye remember what to do once he appears?"

Once, not if. Giles was certain that he would take the bait.

Skye swallowed and nodded. Fear like shards of ice embedded itself in her lungs, and she fought to keep her breathing even. Just the mention of facing him had her breaking out into a sweat.

"I tell him that I Saw his death and would like to propose a trade: Lucas for the time and place."

Giles offered her a kind smile. "It's an irresistible offer for a man like him. He will not be able to refuse ye."

Skye wasn't half as sure, but it was worth a shot if it meant that Lucas could come back to them.

"Shall we begin?" Giles asked, looking around the room.

In turn, each one of them eyed the others before all nodding their agreement. No point in putting this off.

It was time to face the devil.

James grabbed a lighter while Giles went to gather what they needed to cast the circle. Soon, the room filled with the sweet smell of sage. Skye breathed deeply; maybe the sage could work its magic on the negative energy that clung to her.

Moving efficiently, Giles issued orders without taking his eyes off the salt circle he was drawing on the ground.

"Is that really necessary?" James asked.

"Yes," Giles snapped.

James rolled his eyes and muttered something Skye couldn't quite hear.

"You so sure it's not that you want to risk attempting this without it?" she asked him.

"Good point," James said with a frown, his eyes darting to where Lizzie stood a few feet away.

"Alright, James, you're going to stand here at the Northern tip of the circle."

"Any particular reason?" he asked, moving into place where Giles pointed.

"Yer our representation of earth."

"Why, because he's stubborn and unyielding?" Lizzie teased.

Giles grinned while James feigned offense. "I was

thinking more because he is grounded, practical, and quite disciplined."

"See," James said, preening.

"That doesn't mean it was a compliment," Lizzie retorted.

Skye smiled, enjoying their banter even as it made her ache for Lucas. Just weeks ago, it would have been the two of them teasing each other in a similar fashion.

"Lizzie, ye will stand just there. Yes, facing me. Perfect."

Lizzie stood to James' left at a perfect ninety-degree angle and directly across from Giles, who stood to James' right.

It didn't take a rocket scientist to figure out where Skye was supposed to stand. Without waiting for Giles' direction, she moved through the half-circle the others created to stand across from James, thus completing the circle.

"Perfect."

"If I'm earth, what are they?" James asked as he picked up the green candle flickering on the ground beside him.

Skye eyed the white, red, and blue candles. If the elements were tied to the color of their candles, it was pretty obvious. White for air, red for fire, and blue for water. She wasn't certain, but she vaguely remembered hearing that each element was also tied to the four cardinal directions. If earth was North, based on the way they were standing, that meant that air was East, fire was South, and water was West.

Looking at who Giles chose for each place made a certain kind of sense. Skye appreciated the balance, and how well they each represented their chosen element. Lizzie, brilliant, talkative, eternally sweet, was a natural fit for air. Giles, with his wisdom and empathy, was easily water. As for her, fire was tied to creativity and passion. Two things she'd built a life with and often used to describe herself, at least before the Druid had gotten his hands on her. *I'll be those things again.* The silent promise to herself was enough to choke back the pain.

Satisfied, Skye took a deep, centering breath. The more she reflected on it, each person was a practically perfect embodiment of their assigned element, and that small piece of luck helped the tiny flicker of hope inside her burn brighter.

While she'd been lost in thought, Giles had answered James, who currently nodded as if he, too, agreed with her internal assessment.

"Everyone still have the incantation I wrote for them?" Giles asked.

Skye pulled the small piece of paper out of her pocket, even though she'd already memorized the words. Around her, James and Lizzie did the same.

"Good. Then James, start us off."

"Guardians of the North, steadfast and strong, we call on you to protect and help us with our quest." He let some of the dirt he'd grabbed from outside sift through his fingers and fall onto the floor before him.

Knowing her cue, Lizzie took up the chant. "Guardians of the East, ever moving around and through us, we call on you to help keep us on course." She blew gently at the flame of her candle, making it leap and billow before settling back into its happy flicker.

Clearing her throat, Skye said, "Guardians of the South, fierce and kind, we call on you to warm but never burn us." Since her candle was already lit, Skye improvised, feeding the flame by holding her incantation up to it, mesmerized as the flames licked at the piece of paper, quickly turning it to ash.

With a nod of approval, Giles concluded, "Guardians of the West, calm and eternal, we call on you to fill us with your knowledge and perseverance." Taking a small bottle out of his pocket, Giles poured a few drops onto the ground in front of him.

As soon as the first drop hit the floor, all four flames leapt high, tripling in size before settling back into place and a warm gust of air blew through the room.

James' eyes were comically large. He looked like one soft breath would send him toppling over. Lizzie wasn't much better, her eyes furtively scanning the room, her mouth having fallen open in shock.

Skye set her candle down on the table to her right, not trusting herself not to drop it as they continued.

"Are ye ready, lass?" Giles asked Lizzie.

She nodded, setting her own candle aside and wiping her palms on her legs.

"Repeat after me: Reveal and unveil…"

Giles spoke slowly, allowing Lizzie to speak the words mere seconds after he did until it felt as if they spoke in harmony.

"Show me that which I seek. Bring to light what you

keep hidden. Drawn to me like a moth to a flame. Come to me…come to me…come to me…"

There was a ripple in the air, like a blanket being pulled from the bed. The candles blew out, and Skye barely contained her gasp of terror as a cold voice spoke into the darkness.

"Well, well, well, what have we here?"

CHAPTER 19

SKYE

With a hiss, a small ball of light took shape in James' hands, and he lifted the lighter to light the circle. A creepy glow washed over each of their faces, turning them into characters from some kind of horror story told around a campfire.

James stared intently at her from across the circle. The air between them undulated like the top of an otherwise smooth lake. It was the Druid's spirit, nothing more than a transparent apparition. Even still, Skye's body was frozen with fear, and she couldn't quite find the courage to lift her eyes the fraction of an inch higher to determine whether or not the Druid was wearing his hood. James dipped his chin in a slow nod. Her cue to start speaking.

"Miss me already, Seer?"

She settled for staring just over the tip of his right shoulder, but it took three attempts for her to push the words past her lips. "Hardly. I thought you might be interested in hearing some information I've acquired."

The Druid laughed, the sound slithering over her skin.

The tiny hairs lifted on the back of her neck, and she clenched her hands into fists. Everything within her was screaming to flee, but she forced her body to remain still.

"You'll have to do better than that, Skye. Or have you already forgotten how well we know each other now?" His voice was a seductive croon.

Stomach in knots, Skye lifted her shoulder in a careless shrug. "Suit yourself. I just thought you might want to know that I've Seen your future."

Her eyes darted to the place where his face would have been, and she was relieved to find the outline of a hood obscuring it. At least she didn't have to meet those horrible black eyes.

The Druid flickered. Skye hoped it was a sign of his agitation, but she did not let any hint of emotion cross her face. He needed to buy this charade, and she couldn't afford to give anything away.

"I find that hard to believe since I just removed the only obstacle between me and immortality."

Skye tilted her head, copying the movement he'd used on her countless times before. "Did you? Or did you make it so that immortality will be forever just out of reach? If I recall correctly, you had to kill the last remaining Druid in order to acquire his power. What good is he to you if he's still alive while lost to the Wasteland?"

"Are you so eager for his death, Seer?"

She bared her teeth in the smallest imitation of a smile. "Not quite. I just couldn't resist the urge to look you in the eyes when I got to tell you that you failed. You're going to die. You went to all of this trouble, and you still haven't won."

"Bullshit."

"Oh? Then explain the vision to me. You know what my gift is. I have to say, it was the first time a death vision ever brought me quite so much joy. I was smiling when I returned to the present."

"It's true," Lizzie said, her chin tilted defiantly.

The Druid sneered. "I don't believe you."

"As if I care. It doesn't change the future," Skye said. "And now, I can rest a little easier knowing that you'll be haunted by the idea of your death, never knowing when or where it will strike, only that it's coming for you."

Skye started to turn away—

"Wait."

This time, she didn't have to fake her grin. "What?"

"Tell me what you Saw."

"No."

"No? Then why call me here, Seer?"

"So I could watch you squirm, you pathetic piece of shit. You may have torn me apart piece by piece, both my body and my heart, but you will never win. Death will find you. And when it does, I am going to dance on your grave."

"I can still make your life a living hell while I'm alive, Seer. Do you not realize our time apart has been a gift? I could easily come for you and slit your throat in your sleep. Have you forgotten the last time I visited your dreams?"

Icy sweat rolled down her back, but Skye clung tooth and nail to her rage. "I dare you to try."

"Skye—" Lizzie warned, her voice low but obviously frightened.

"Listen to my granddaughter, little Seer."

Skye grit her teeth. "You want the details, asshole? It's going to cost you, and I'm willing to bet it's a price you're not going to want to pay."

"Money is no object."

"Who said anything about money? If I give this to you, I want it to hurt."

"What do you want?" he asked, his voice an angry crack.

"Tell me how you got out of the Wasteland."

He let out a bark of laughter. "That's your price? What could you possibly do with that information?"

"Why don't you leave that to me."

"You're a bigger fool than I thought if you think you can go after him."

Skye shrugged. "I never said I was going to."

"Then why?"

"You don't need to know. That's not our bargain, Druid."

She could feel the weight of his gaze boring into her, but she didn't flinch, even though her heart pounded inside its cage. *Please buy it. Please buy it. Please,* it begged with each thumping beat.

"Fine," he growled. "But you tell me first—"

"No deal," she said, cutting him off. "I don't trust you to tell me after you get what you need."

"And why should I trust you?"

"That's not my problem. I'm just as happy watching you dangle like the worm you are."

The crackle of James' lighter and Giles' shallow breaths were the only sounds in the room as the Druid considered her offer.

"The way out of the Wasteland is the same as the way in. Sacrifice. An equal exchange. The Wasteland will accept nothing less."

"What the fuck does that mean?" James demanded.

"A soul price," Giles whispered, understanding what none of the rest of them did.

The Druid ignored them. "I gave you what you wanted, Seer. Now, it's your turn."

"You were standing inside of a stone circle. The night was clear, starless. Three hooded figures stepped into the circle, one pulled a runed dagger from within the folds of their cloak. There was a blast of light, the figure fell, but the other two reached you. You fought. When all three had fallen, you thought you won. You never saw the one that remained hidden. They struck while you were busy defiling the corpses of the others. I would tell you it was quick, but it wasn't. Whoever's going to kill you wants you to suffer." Skye let her hatred shine as she started at his spirit form. "I hope they succeed, you miserable bastard. A quick death is far too kind for you."

"Who were they?" the Druid demanded.

"I told you all I Saw. Rot in hell, asshole," Skye sneered, turning and walking away from where he remained inside of their circle.

"Seer! Get back here, you stupid bitch."

Skye kept walking even though her legs shook. She didn't stop moving until she was out of the room and locked inside Lucas' bedroom. Only then did she allow herself to slide to the floor and heave.

She was still trembling when James found her.

"You did so good, Skye. Lucas would be proud of you."

Wiping a hand over her mouth, Skye looked up from where she was huddled on the floor. "Is he gone?"

James nodded.

Relief chased away some of the fear, but she was still too light-headed to stand. "Good."

"Can I get you anything?"

"Water?" she asked.

"You got it."

Before he walked out the door, Skye called to him. "James?"

"Yeah?" he asked, twisting back around to face her.

"What do you think a soul price is?"

James' smile faltered, and he shook his head. "I'm not sure, but Giles seemed to know. When you're feeling better, we will ask him. Just rest now, okay? You've done enough for today."

"It's not enough until we get him back," she insisted.

"And we will. Let's deal with one thing at a time, alright?"

Skye wanted to argue, but the emotional toll of the day had all but drained her, and she couldn't ignore the wisdom of his words. It required more effort than it should just for her to remain sitting upright. She really had pushed herself. Skye cursed her weakness, but nodded in agreement.

James left, and Skye managed to crawl into the bed. She pulled the blankets that still smelled faintly of Lucas over her and then leaned back against the pillows, letting the softness of them absorb some of her tension.

After closing her eyes, she pictured Lucas, his cocky grin, and even the ridiculous unicorn tattoo on his ass.

With a smile of her own, Skye drifted off. *We're coming, Lucas*.

CHAPTER 20

LUCAS

"Lizzie, would you just back off already?" Lucas stared down the woman standing in front of him with her hands braced on her hips. Somewhere in the back of his mind, he knew it wasn't actually his sister, but the part that recognized the difference between reality and the Wasteland's tricks slipped away more each and every single day.

"I'm just saying, you aren't going to find anything here."

Lucas pressed his hands to his ears to drown out the sound of her incessant whining.

"Don't waste your breath, Lizzie. You know what a stubborn ass he is," Skye interjected from her post against the side of the cavern. She leaned against a rune-covered wall, inspecting her nails.

Ignoring them both, Lucas focused on the drawings he'd been studying. Part of him wanted to slide down to the ground, allow himself to forget that none of this was real, and simply accept his fate.

But the small piece of him that remembered his true family, the part of him who knew they were in danger, stubbornly refused to let him give up.

"Come on, baby." Skye left her post and pressed up against him. "Don't you want me? Don't you want us to be together, just like old times?"

Closing his eyes, he pretended he couldn't feel the heat of her body where it was molded against his. The way her breasts rose and fell with each breath as if she were actually alive.

Barely resisting, Lucas shook his head. "You aren't real. My Skye is waiting for me."

"Is she?" Skye pouted. "Because I'd be willing to bet she's already in bed with the Druid. He *is* more powerful than you."

White-hot rage shot through him, pulling him just far enough back from the edge of madness that he shoved her away and glared down at her. "If you aren't going to leave me the fuck alone, then shut the hell up."

Wasteland Skye sulked, her bottom lip in a full sexy pout, but Lucas couldn't care less. He turned his attention back to the markings on the wall. They were all so familiar, and yet, his mind couldn't grasp the meaning of any of them.

What was the fucking point of having power when you couldn't use it? He'd drawn all of the symbols he knew, tried every single spell in his mind, and nothing had worked. He'd even used the sharp edge of one of the rocks to slice through his palm.

Not even his Druid blood sparked any power.

Since being here, he hadn't been able to call up a

single flicker of actual magic. Unless he counted what he could still feel beating against his veins like an over-flowing dam about to burst. Which reiterated his initial question: what was the point?

How the hell had that bastard escaped the Wasteland? What spell—or combination of spells—had he used to get back? Was it possible someone found a way to pull him from this place?

What if it had been Giles? And now, he was working with Lizzie and Skye!

Lucas closed his eyes as images of his real sister and a bloody and broken Skye popped into his mind.

"No, no, no. *Not* Giles. He's been helping us," Lucas said.

"Has he though?" Lizzie asked.

Lucas slapped himself, one sharp crack against his cheek. The stinging pain worked to snap himself back to reality. Well, if not actual reality, it at least helped remind him what was true.

"I can do that for you," Skye offered. "If you're into it."

Lucas glared at her until she put up both her hands and took a couple of shuffling steps back. With a sigh, he turned back to the wall. *Treat it like a crime scene, MacConnell.* The problem was, he already had. He'd combed every single inch of the cave and found nothing other than the blade made from rock, and these fucking runes.

"The Druid escaped from here," Lizzie reminded him.

"Well, he's more powerful than you'll ever be," Wasteland Skye taunted.

Both of the mirage women laughed.

"Too bad you weren't man enough to save me," Skye added, twisting the verbal dagger she'd just gutted him with.

Lucas spun, pinning Skye to the wall. Her eyes stuck him with a steely gaze, so unlike the warm, loving woman he'd known.

"Are we finally doing this then?" She ran her hand over his bicep, and his traitorous body shivered at her touch.

"I'll give you two some privacy." Lizzie disappeared with a knowing grin.

Skye arched up against him, her breasts pressing into the arm across her throat. "What are you waiting for, Detective?"

Breaking his number one rule of the Wasteland, Lucas leaned down and crushed his mouth to hers. The kiss was bruising and mean. He poured every ounce of his frustration into the kiss, hoping to punish Skye for fucking with his mind. Even the illusion of passion was enough to have his cock hardening in anticipation, and it was no longer clear exactly who Lucas was punishing.

He slanted his mouth over hers to deepen the kiss, his hips pressing into her welcoming body in an attempt to alleviate the ache. Hands tangling in her hair, Lucas lost himself in the kiss.

A familiar copper tang filled his mouth, and he jerked away, coughing and spitting up blood.

Skye grinned at him, looking like some kind of demented vampire with crimson smears on her lips and chin. "Poor Detective. Can't handle it, can you?" Skye wiped the back of her hand against her mouth, taking the blood with it.

Lucas gasped for air, fighting the urge to vomit. There was nothing in his stomach, and he knew from experience it would only lead to a day of dry heaving.

"Can you imagine what he did to me?" Skye asked, her amber eyes wild. "All because you weren't man enough to save me!"

Lucas covered his ears. Pain, raw and fresh, ripped through his body, dropping him to his knees.

"Lizzie, you can come back now," Skye sang, a satisfied smirk on her once again pristine face.

"Fuck!" Lucas roared, slamming his fist into the wall. "Son of a bitch!" He yanked his hand back, studying the split and bloody knuckles.

"Great, now you fucking broke it, dumbass," Lizzie scolded him.

"Leave me alone!" Lucas screamed. "Get the fuck out of my head!" Lucas clutched his throbbing—probably broken—hand, cradling it against his chest.

"We're coming, Lucas."

The words were spoken softly, lovingly, which was not even remotely fitting for the mirages he'd been living with. Lucas whipped around to stare down the impostor Skye.

"What the hell did you just say?"

She threw Lizzie an amused grin and then turned back to him. "Hearing voices now, are you? Sounds like you might just be losing your mind…"

"How fun," Lizzie said, giggling.

Lucas shook his head. He'd heard the words. They'd been as clear as if they'd been spoken directly into his ear.

He slapped himself again, something he was having to do more frequently than he cared to admit. It was the only way to keep his thoughts straight.

"Wow, he really is a goner," Lizzie commented.

Using some of his blood, he drew the symbol for healing on his injured hand. Knowing it was futile, he uttered the activation word.

The blood and pain remained. Lucas swallowed back a groan.

"We're coming, Lucas." The words radiated through his mind, giving him hope.

Even if they weren't true, even if the promise had been just another trick of his mind, Lucas got to his feet. The real Skye, Lizzie, and Matthews were waiting back in Scotland, and they were counting on him.

"This won't last long," Skye commented.

"Never does," Lizzie added with a yawn.

Lucas reached forward and touched the symbol closest to him with his fingertips. It was the largest of all the runes and looked like it might also be the newest. The color was less diminished than the others.

Was it possible that this was the way home? Maybe a portal of some kind? Glancing at his injured hand, Lucas dipped a finger in the still wet blood.

After a brief hesitation and silent plea that he wasn't about to make things even worse for himself, Lucas traced the rune with his own blood.

Once it was done, he closed his eyes and murmured the Gaelic word for home, "*Dachaigh*."

Silence swelled around him; there wasn't even the

buzz of insects to fill the beats while Lucas waited. Defeated, Lucas opened his eyes.

"Wait! That didn't work? I wonder why!" Skye exclaimed, and she and Lizzie both broke into a fit of uncontrollable laughter.

"Probably used the wrong word, dumbass," Lizzie wheezed.

His face heated with embarrassment, and Lucas stomped from the cave. He'd said the first word that came to mind. Instinct had always served him well, but everything was fucked here. Maybe his imaginary sister was right. It's not like he could even trust what he was seeing in this place.

Lucas sat down in the sand and stared out at the sea of nothing before him. If the answer wasn't here, then where the hell was it?

CHAPTER 21

SKYE

After spending the early morning following her Gran's advice and revisiting her non-death visions, Skye stretched and rolled out of bed, placing both feet on the ground. A feat that had become easier the last two days. She wriggled her toes down into the thick carpet and allowed herself a soft smile.

Lucas was alive, and he was waiting for them. She could feel the truth of it in her bones.

Pushing to her feet, Skye pulled on a pair of jeans and a red sweatshirt. Without bothering to make use of the mirror, Skye pulled her mass of hair over her shoulder and braided the length so that it concealed the bulk of the bandage around her ear. She found it easier to be among the others when they weren't constantly reminded of her injury. The pitying glances made it hard for her to focus. And right now, she only had one thing on her mind: bringing Lucas back.

She left the room, following the alluring scent of freshly brewed coffee to the kitchen. She was happy to see both Lizzie and James sitting at the small table, enjoying steaming mugs. Soon, Lucas would be here to enjoy it with them, too.

"Morning," Skye greeted with a smile.

"How are you doing?" Lizzie asked with a cautious smile of her own.

It shamed her that they automatically assumed she would be broken, that she would be destroyed this morning because she'd been forced to see and speak with the Druid last night. Not that she'd given them any reason to think otherwise; forty-eight hours ago, she *had* been broken, on the verge of a complete and total breakdown, all by the mere illusion of him.

Now, though, she felt stronger, each day further cementing her hope that soon, Lucas would be home, and they could get back to living again. Well, once they dealt with the Druid. But even that would be easier once Lucas returned.

"I'm okay," Skye assured them, pouring herself a mug and sitting down in one of the empty chairs.

"Any nightmares?" James took a sip of his coffee, his eyes never leaving her face.

"Nope, not one." And that was the truth. For the first time since her kidnapping, she'd had an entirely dreamless, restful night of sleep.

It felt damn good.

"Glad to hear it," Lizzie said with a smile.

"Did you guys talk any more about what the Druid meant when he said leaving the Wasteland required a sacrifice? What did Giles call it, a soul price?"

James shook his head. "Giles took off pretty quick afterwards, said he needed to think about it."

Lizzie stared down into her mug, worry turning her eyes a stormy blue. "It can't mean a life, can it? Otherwise, the Druid wouldn't have been able to get himself back."

"It sounds like a life to me. What else would classify as a soul price?" James asked.

Lizzie's shoulders slumped with his assessment, and she began to fiddle with her coffee mug.

"I'm not so sure," Skye said.

Lizzie and James' eyes darted over to her, and her shoulders lifted defensively under the weight of their joint stares.

"I mean…you're right, it *could* mean a life, but what if it literally refers to giving up your soul?"

Lizzie gaped at her. "Is that even possible?"

"Think about it…if it takes a life to send someone to the Wasteland, it seems logical the soul would be sent there as well. What if sacrificing a life means that the soul is also trapped? If the Druid found a way to sacrifice your grandmother's soul from *inside* the Wasteland, maybe that's how he got back?"

"Maybe…" Lizzie said, but she sounded far from sure.

"The Druid does seem like a soulless bastard, maybe it was his soul he parted with," James chimed in.

"That seems more likely," Lizzie muttered.

Skye couldn't disagree. "Either way, we need to get started. The longer Lucas is stuck there, the worse it's going to be for him."

Getting to her feet, Skye carried her now empty mug to the sink. James and Lizzie followed suit, the trio growing silent as they rinsed out their cups, the seriousness of the ritual they were about to perform taking hold.

The only way for a non-Druid to send someone to the Wasteland required a living sacrifice. Maggie, Lucas and Lizzie's grandmother, had paid that price when she and Giles trapped Oliver there. In order for them to get to Lucas, one of them had to do the same. Giles still insisted it should be him.

Just as they entered the living room, the front door opened, and Giles walked inside. It was a testament to how comfortable they'd become with each other that he no longer knocked or waited for someone to let him in. They'd become a tightly knit unit in their fight against the Druid. A family, really. Which only made what they had to do today that much harder.

"Morning, Giles," Skye greeted.

He returned her smile, but there were purple smudges beneath his eyes. It was obvious he hadn't slept at all last night. Seeing as how he was planning on giving his life today, that wasn't much of a surprise.

"Morning, lass, feeling well?"

"I am, thanks." She was about to ask how he was feeling and then thought better of it.

"Good, good." Shifting his focus to the others, he said, "I think the Druid may have used Maggie's soul to get out of the Wasteland."

"That's what Skye thinks, too," James said.

"Oh?"

"It couldn't have been a life, right, since we're assuming Maggie was dead when she got there? But if leaving requires paying some kind of soul price, then it could be he figured out a way to use hers as a means of escape," Skye explained, folding her arms.

"That's so awful," Lizzie said, her voice cracking at the end. "To not only be the reason someone is dead but to also be the reason that their soul will never move on to whatever is next. It's absolutely horrifying."

"That it is, lass," Giles said sadly. "As we know, the Druid is not much for sentiment, so it's not that far of a reach to believe him capable of such atrocity." Giles reached into the leather bag hanging from his shoulder and pulled out an old leather-bound book and a runed dagger.

"What are those?" James asked.

"The items Maggie and I used to send Oliver away. The spells are all in that book, and this is the—" His voice broke as he ran his finger over the silver blade. "This is the dagger Maggie used to kill herself."

"Are you sure you want to do this?" Lizzie reached forward and touched his trembling hand. "We can find another way."

Giles looked up at her, a tear falling down his wrinkled cheek. "I appreciate that, but we all know there is no other way. A life must be sacrificed to open the portal to the Wasteland, and since I helped send Oliver there in the first place, it should be mine." He patted her hand. "I've come to terms with my future, lass."

Silvery tears shimmered in her eyes as Lizzie stepped back. James wrapped an arm around her shoulders, offering his strength and support.

Skye swallowed hard. After today, their group—their family—of five would be permanently back down to four.

Taking the blade from Giles, Skye kissed his cheek.

She set it aside and turned back to him. "Let's focus on getting these runes painted so we can bring Lucas home."

Giles smiled softly, moss-green eyes crinkling. "Sounds like a fine plan."

Using red paint, the four went to work copying the runes from his book onto the walls. With each stroke of her brush, a sense of peace settled over Skye. Between her Gran's visit in her dream, and what the Druid had told them, she knew what had to be done and was ready for what it would mean for her and for their future.

"I say, those are the best-looking runes I've ever seen," Giles said with a smile, setting down his brush.

"I agree. We kick ass," Lizzie responded, surveying the finished project.

Skye swapped her wet paint brush for Giles' runed dagger. "Ready?" she asked him.

Giles let out a breath. "I am. Maybe I'll see Maggie on the other side."

James patted him on the shoulder. "I bet you will, man."

Skye moved into the center of the room and studied the runes on the wall. "What do we have to do next?"

"We need blood on the runes."

"Can it be anyone's blood?" Skye asked.

"Aye, but 'tis better if Lizzie does it, since hers has the best chance of containing power out of all of us."

"Lucky me," Lizzie said dryly. "Go ahead, Skye. You do the honors."

Skye turned over Lizzie's hand, and with a mumbled apology, she sliced into Lizzie's palm.

"Fuck, that hurts!"

"Baby," James teased.

Lizzie glared at him. "Who you callin' a baby?" she asked, holding her dripping palm up to his face.

James blanched. After all he'd seen, he still couldn't quite stomach the sight of blood. Swallowing, he held up his hands and backed away from her. "I just meant that Lucas does it all the time, and he doesn't complain."

"Because that makes it better," Lizzie said, rolling her eyes. Moving away from him, she walked around the room and pressed her palm to the center of each glistening rune.

Skye's thundering pulse made it impossible to hear much over her own heartbeat.

"My turn," Giles said once Lizzie had finished.

Wrapping her arms around him, Lizzie spoke through her tears, "Thank you, Giles."

Tuning them out, Skye moved back to the center of the room, a note for Lucas in her pocket, and the blade clutched in her hand. She should have been scared, but she wasn't. Her Gran had been right. She'd always held the answer. Maggie was the one who'd shown her what needed to be done. There was only ever one way the curse would be broken. It just so happened that it would also be what set Lucas free.

"Thank you, guys, for everything you've done for me," Skye said, her voice barely more than a whisper.

Three sets of eyes turned to her.

"What did you say?" Lizzie asked, her eyes widening as she realized what was about to happen. "Skye, no!" she screamed.

Lizzie lunged for the dagger, but Skye had already plunged the blade into her chest. Pain surged through her, searing her body with a fire so hot it sent a shiver down her spine as death's icy embrace wrapped itself around her and called her home. Skye gasped around the pain, her fingers falling lifelessly to her sides. She fell to her knees, the blade protruding grotesquely from her body.

Time seemed to slow as she stared up at the horrified faces of Giles, Lizzie, and James. James slid to the ground beside her, catching her just as she fell back.

"Why, Skye? You can't do this!" Lizzie screamed. "Do something!" she yelled at Giles.

"I-I can't," Giles babbled. "The runes are already active—"

"It has to be me," Skye choked out. "Don't you see? It's the only way—" she broke off as blood bubbled in her throat.

Her vision swam as a numbing calm settled in. *That's nice.* No longer feeling any pain, Skye stared up at the ceiling, trying to listen to what was going on around her. Somewhere in the distance, Giles told the others that they had to move away from her body, to leave her, but the chattering turned to static as a bright white light filled the room, and her eyes fluttered closed.

CHAPTER 22

SKYE

Skye bat at her cheek, trying to brush off whatever was tickling her. Feeling the rough scratch of sand beneath her fingers, she opened her eyes.

"Where-where am I?" she asked, slowly pushing herself into a sitting position.

A careful look around told her she definitely wasn't in Scotland anymore. Was this a vision, then? The muted gray shades of all that surrounded her almost had the same feel, although the sky had never looked quite like this before… like nail polish that had dripped out of the bottle and was absorbing the new drops in an endless collection of ever-widening rings.

If it was a vision, there should be people, right? There always had been before. But she was utterly alone. *Not a vision, then.*

She glanced down, taking in her attire to see if that provided any clues. Jeans and a tattered red sweatshirt with a hole in the center. *When did that happen?* She reached up to touch the cleanly sliced edges as if they held the answer.

Skye gasped as soon as her fingers made contact, feeling the phantom sting of a blade sliding through her chest.

The memories assaulted her then. The dagger. The runes. Her sacrifice.

If she was dead, then that meant this must be…well, certainly not Heaven. There was a decided lack of pearly gates. But it didn't look like Hell either; not a trace of fire or brimstone to be found. Purgatory, then?

Skye stood up, not seeing anything but endless mounds of sand in every direction. *Great.* She sacrificed herself and got sent to an eternal desert to live out the rest of her…afterlife?

Letting out a little huff, Skye did the only thing she could think of: she walked.

"You're never going to get anywhere unless the land wants you to," a woman called.

Skye froze, her eyes scanning the horizon in search of the speaker.

"It's fickle that way, just like the men that created it."

A tingle started at the base of her neck. The speaker was behind her. Hesitating only because she wasn't sure whether the speaker was a friend or a foe, Skye was slow to turn around. Until she remembered. *She can't hurt you, dummy. You're already dead.* That was going to take some getting used to.

The woman had some kind of scarf wrapped around her face to ward off the small gusts of sand that the wind kept flinging into the air. All Skye could make out from where she stood was that the woman was about a head taller than her and had light eyes.

"So, what? I just stand still and do nothing forever?"

The woman shrugged. “That’s certainly one way to pass the time. Once the land gets a sense of you, it will determine your fate.”

“The land?”

The woman gestured to the sand around them. “The Wasteland.”

Skye’s heart gave a painful lurch before its tempo increased and it began to race. “Wha-what did you just say?”

“Welcome to the Wasteland, sweetheart. Population, two.”

“Two?” Skye asked, her heart plummeting to her feet. Then that meant…had Lucas not survived after all?

The woman pointed to herself and then Skye as if the math should have been obvious.

Licking her lips, Skye asked, “Is it possible that there are others you simply haven’t found yet?”

She tilted her head as she considered the question. “It’s possible. I cannae claim to know all of its secrets.”

Her relief was almost as painful as the thought of Lucas being gone forever. Legs folding beneath her, Skye sat down hard in the sand. “Forgive me, I just need a minute.”

“By all means,” the woman said, “it’s not like we have anything but time.”

Questions flew through her mind, each one colliding with another, demanding to be asked first. *Who was she? How did she get here? Who were the men that created this place? Had she met Lucas? Oliver? Did she know what the soul price was? Why was Skye sent here, but not one of the others?*

"I'm Maggie, by the way," the woman said, answering the first of her unspoken questions. "And who might ye be?"

Maggie. Shock rendered her momentarily speechless, and then Skye laughed. "You're Lucas' grandmother." *Of course.*

The woman took a tentative step forward, her brows furrowed. "Ye know my grandson?"

"Know him? Yeah, I would say I know him."

Maggie closed the distance between them and dropped to her knees in front of Skye. "Why did he send ye here?" she demanded, her pleasantly casual voice going cold.

Even though all Skye could see was the muted color of Maggie's eyes, there was no mistaking the resemblance to Lizzie and Lucas.

"Lucas didn't send me here. I came here to bring him home, well—" Skye stopped, trying to figure out how to best explain what had happened.

When she'd decided to be the one to offer herself up, she hadn't quite planned on waking up on the other side. She had thought Giles or maybe Lizzie would be pulled through in her place. That had been their plan, initially. Giles would make the sacrifice, and she would be sent through, just like Maggie and Oliver had been so many years ago. And sure, Giles suspected Maggie might have made it, but Skye never really believed it was possible. Dead was dead…

Well, apparently, that wasn't true either.

Maybe it would be easiest if she started with something simpler. "I'm Skye Giovanni," she announced, holding out her hand.

Her eyes grew distant, and her voice thoughtful. "Giovanni. I know that name."

"My Gran once helped you and Giles."

"How do ye know about that?"

"I have visions."

"Yer a Gypsy like your Gran."

Skye nodded. "Giles helped me figure out how to get here."

Maggie's eyes softened. "He's alive?"

"Yes, but…the Druid—Oliver—escaped."

"I know, bastard made me watch him leave. I'd feared he was going back to kill Giles."

"Not Giles. He went after Lucas and Lizzie."

Maggie covered her mouth with a hand. "Did he—are they alive?"

"They are, but Lucas is trapped here. I came hoping he'd find me and read this." She pulled a note from her pocket and held it out to Maggie.

"Escaping requires a soul price," she read aloud. "How did ye find this out?"

Skye's smile turned smug. "I tricked the Druid—Oliver —into telling me."

"I can't imagine he gave that information freely." Maggie reached forward and brushed the hair back from Skye's bandaged ear. "Did he do that?"

Covering it with her hair again, Skye nodded. "I told him I Saw his death."

Maggie chuckled. "And why would he believe that? Oliver was never daft…or has he changed?"

"You're familiar with my Gran's gift?"

Maggie nodded.

"I'm a Seer just like she was."

"Ah, yes, that would do it then." Maggie studied Skye. "You say my grandson is here?"

"Yes."

"How long has he been here?"

"Just over a week."

Unwinding the wrap from her head, she shifted until she was sitting beside Skye. Sighing, she said, "I felt a surge of power; even without having magic of my own, I can sense it in here. It's why I have been wandering. I was waiting to see if perhaps Giles found a way to send Oliver back." She looked up at the sun. "We need to find Lucas, and soon. If he's been here over a week, he doesn't have much time left."

"What do you mean?"

"This place absorbs power, Skye. 'Tis why it is such a horrid place for a Druid to be trapped. It takes decades for the deterioration to begin, but mere weeks for insanity to set in. If Lucas is here, 'tis possible he's already too far gone to save. Although, I hope his brand will help buy him time."

"His brand? You mean that rune on his side? You know about that?"

"Who do ye think gave it to him?" she asked.

"I thought you said you didn't have power?"

"No, but my son does."

Skye stood, brushing sand off her back and legs. Holding out a hand to help Maggie stand, she said, "Lucas is strong. I don't believe it's too late to save him."

"I pray ye're right, dear."

Not looking where she was going, Skye stumbled in

the sand, but managed to recover before falling. Maggie was more used to navigating through the dunes, and Skye did her best to keep up with her quick pace.

"My son used to take my grandchildren camping. Lucas would know to seek shelter. I know a place where he might be."

"You've been here for decades. How have you not gone insane?"

"Who says I haven't?" Maggie asked with a smile.

Skye grinned. "You seem so much like the woman I Saw in my vision."

"I am not magical; this place only draws on power."

"I don't understand how you're alive—how I'm alive."

"Ye were healed by the gateway. It's not yer life that this place wants, Skye, 'tis your soul."

A soul price. A soul sacrifice. "A permanent prison."

"Aye."

They continued walking, and while Maggie was not much of a talker, Skye kept stealing glances at the woman every chance she got. Lizzie favored her grandmother immensely, bright blue eyes and beautiful golden hair, although Maggie's was liberally streaked with gray. Even the shape of their noses was identical.

"How is my son?"

Skye winced. Of course she wouldn't have known. "I'm afraid he passed away."

Maggie stopped, spinning to face her. "Oliver?"

"No, car accident. He and his wife both died."

Maggie pressed a hand to her heart, tears filling her blue eyes. "I know they've thought me dead a long time, but I'd always imagined them alive and happy."

"I'm so sorry, Maggie. From what Lizzie and Lucas have told me, they were very happy up until the end."

Maggie squeezed her hand. Skye returned the grasp while Maggie cleared her throat and wiped her cheeks. "We need to focus on Lucas now. I'll have plenty of time to grieve them later."

They started walking again, and Skye practically jogged to keep up. Her short legs were no match for Maggie's long stride.

"How far is this place?" Skye asked.

"Depends on whether the Wasteland wants to mess with yer mind or not. When it's draining power, it prefers ye to be in the open, making ye an easier target for its sandstorms and hallucinations."

"And if it doesn't?"

"If it doesn't, we should be coming up on the cave shortly."

They continued their walk in silence, and Skye couldn't fight back her growing excitement. Being trapped in the Wasteland aside, she was closer to Lucas than she'd been in weeks. Ever since the day the Druid had kidnapped her.

To see him again—even if it was only for a moment before he had to leave—it would be more than enough to make her sacrifice worth it.

Then he could go on to kill the Druid and save Lizzie and James. There would be no more suffering for her friends, and she could live the rest of eternity in this place knowing she'd done all she could for them.

"So, what are ye to my grandson?" Maggie asked.

"What do you mean?"

"You sacrificed your life for him"—the woman raised her eyebrows—"I'm assuming there's a reason."

Skye swallowed hard. "I love him. I can't think of a better reason than that."

"No, I don't imagine there is one." Maggie stopped. "Loving a Druid 'tis not an easy task, is it?"

"It certainly hasn't been so far. Then again, we've been running from Oliver since day one."

"I'm sorry, Skye. For all the suffering Oliver has caused ye."

"No need to apologize. It wasn't your fault." Skye started walking again, desperate to find Lucas.

They crested the top of a sandy hill, and just below, Skye saw the opening to a cave.

"Is that it?"

"Aye. 'Tis where Oliver sought refuge as well."

Skye started down the hill, heart pounding in her chest with each sliding step. As she reached the bottom, she broke into a run, stopping just before she walked inside to look back at Maggie. The woman made her way down more slowly, and gestured for Skye to go ahead.

Grateful the older woman wouldn't make her wait even a few minutes longer, Skye took a deep breath and crossed the threshold into the inky darkness of the cave. "Lucas?"

"Fuck off and die!" he yelled, and all trace of her excitement dissipated as if someone had popped a giant balloon.

"Lucas, it's Skye." She walked further inside and spotted him sitting in a corner, his back against the damp stone.

He didn't bother looking up. "I'm sure it is. Here to torture me some more?"

Since she knew what a dagger to the heart felt like now, it was an accurate description for the pain his words caused. Only Maggie's warning that the Wasteland liked to play tricks kept her moving forward.

"I'm not here to torture you, I came to save you."

Lucas lifted his head, and his eyes glared at her with blue fire. Skye offered him a tentative smile. He was dirty, and currently looked like he wanted to rip her head off, but he was whole, and the most beautiful thing she'd ever seen.

He got to his feet, stalking toward her.

"I've missed you," Skye stammered.

"Have you? Couldn't have been more than ten minutes since I saw you last. You were telling me all about what a fuck up I was. How I let you down and left you at the mercy of that bastard. How you were spreading your legs for him now because he was so much more powerful than I am."

Skye backed up, the chilling hatred in his eyes sending panic through her veins. Was he already gone?

"Lucas, look at me. It's me. Twyla." Her back hit the stone, and Lucas wrapped his fingers around her throat.

Her use of the nickname only seemed to enrage him further. His nostrils flared, and his eyes narrowed on her face. "You know what, I'm getting to the point where I really don't fucking care whether you're real or not. How about we fuck? That's what you want from me, right? Will that get you to finally leave me the fuck alone?"

He crushed his mouth to hers, and Skye groaned.

Angry or not, feeling his body pressed up against hers was a gift. Skye couldn't get enough. She melted into him, wrapping her body around his, trying to pull him closer. She threaded her fingers through his hair, while her other hand cradled his cheek.

Lucas froze at her tender caress, pulling away to really look at her for the first time. "Skye?" The hatred that had burned in his eyes was gone. "Is it really you?" he asked, his voice breaking as his eyes filled with tears.

She nodded, unable to speak.

Lucas removed his hand and pushed the hair back from the bandage on the side of her head. Her heart stammered in her chest as she held her breath. Would he think she was ugly now? Would he hate what she'd become?

"It really is you," he whispered, his grief-stricken eyes breaking her heart as he gently stroked the edges of her bandage.

Lucas pulled her against his body and wrapped his arms around her. Skye held on, her shoulders shaking as she sobbed against his chest.

"Fuck, Skye. How did you get here? Why did you come?" He pulled back just far enough to look down at her face, still holding onto her arms.

"I—"

"She sacrificed herself to save ye."

Maggie stepped into the cavern, and Lucas' jaw dropped.

"Nan?"

"'Tis wonderful to see you again, Lucas. 'Tis been a long time."

CHAPTER 23

LUCAS

Still gripping Skye's arms, Lucas stared into the eyes of a dead woman. Or at least, a woman he'd long believed dead. Crystal blue eyes stared back at him, crinkling in the corners as a slight grin spread on her face.

"Nan?" he asked again, still unsure she was real. Had this fucking place found another way to screw with him?

"Aye, Lucas." Her eyes filled with tears.

Lucas released Skye, taking a lurching step toward his grandmother. "How is this possible? How are you even here?"

"I never left."

The words cut through the remaining pieces of disbelief, and Lucas rushed toward her, pulling the old woman against him in a tight embrace. They clung to each other, tears streaming down both of their faces while memories of childhood visits filled his mind. Lucas released her, stepping back so that he could see her face.

"I-I can't believe it. It's so good to see you, Nan. We

hoped that you somehow survived the trip, that maybe the Druid—I mean Pop—would have saved you."

She shook her head, a shadow crossing her otherwise bright eyes. "He did not."

"Then how?"

"The gateway did. 'Tis pure magic. I was healed by the time I woke up. Much like your Skye, it would seem."

Lucas shot Skye a look, but she wouldn't meet his gaze. Leaving that conversation for another time, Lucas turned back to his Nan. "The horrible things he must have put you through while you were trapped here together."

She shrugged. "Honestly, it was worth it knowing he wasn't out there to hurt ye and yer dad."

Lucas inwardly groaned. He was going to have to tell her sooner or later. "Nan, about dad—"

Her smile was sad. "It's okay, Lucas. I already know." His confusion must have shown because she added, "Skye told me."

Lucas looked back at Skye, who stood with her arms wrapped around her body. She looked so slight standing there, more doll than grown woman. Her cheeks were gaunt, and her body was more angles than curves. She'd clearly lost a lot of weight—weight she couldn't afford to lose in the first place. Her hair had lost most of its luster, and her eyes were darker now, filled with the shadows of all she'd been through. She looked unwell, like she should be in a hospital bed hooked up to a number of beeping machines, a fact he'd somehow overlooked in his shock that she was really here.

What the hell had she gone through those weeks they were apart?

"I'm going to step outside and give you two a few moments." Patting his shoulder, his Nan wrapped her shawl over her face and stepped outside.

Silence stretched between them as he stared at the woman who'd ripped his heart to shreds. Even with the lost time, the pain was still so raw and fresh that she could have left the note for him only days ago.

Was it unfair that a part of him was still angry about the words she'd written?

"What happened to your hand?" she asked, gesturing to his bruised and swollen knuckles. He looked down; he'd completely forgotten about it in the shock of seeing her again.

"Got into a fight with a rock."

"A rock?"

Lucas nodded. "You should see the other guy."

Skye snorted, a small smile playing at her lips. After a few moments of silence, it disappeared.

"I'm sorry," she said softly, looking down at her hands before shifting her eyes back to his face.

"For?"

"The note."

Lucas folded his arms. They were going to have to have this conversation sooner or later. Better they got everything out on the table now. "So, he didn't force you to write it, then?"

Skye shook her head, a tear slipping down her cheek. Staring over his shoulder, she sucked in a shaky breath before turning those amber eyes back on him. "I Saw my death."

"And decided to run away to try and avoid it?" The

anger he'd managed to keep from his voice so far finally slipped in. Had she really tried to run away because she was scared?

Skye flinched. "No, it wasn't like that. The Druid killed me in front of you, knowing what it would do to you. Watching me die changed you, Lucas. It turned you into someone—something—else. You murdered James, Lucas. I couldn't let that happen."

Disbelief cut through him. "You know I would never do anything to hurt him."

Skye took a step toward him, her voice pleading for him to understand. "I know you wouldn't. But after Seeing that, after knowing that my visions *always* come true…I had to try"—her voice broke on the word—"I had to keep it from happening, even if it meant destroying myself in the process."

"Destroying you? What the hell do you think it did to me, Skye? To think you left me behind? That you threw what we had away…"

More tears slipped down her cheeks. Skye hastily brushed them away, her voice trembling as she asked, "Had?"

Lucas stared at her. Hearing the truth behind her note and why she'd tried to leave made it easier to deal with the anger eating him from the inside, but it only made his guilt grow. She'd left to protect them and suffered greatly for it. He couldn't bear to watch her suffer further.

"Have," he whispered, taking a step toward her.

When she smiled, a piece of himself slipped back into place. Lucas' heart ached; his next words would wipe her smile away again. But he had to know.

"What did he do to you?" he asked softly, brushing her hair back to reveal the bandage covering the side of her head.

Skye closed her eyes and shook her head. "Lucas, please. I don't want to talk about it."

"Skye, look at me."

Her chest rose and fell several times before she opened her eyes and looked up at him.

"I'm so fucking sorry for what you went through."

"I know." It was all she could manage to say before her face crumpled and her tears broke free.

Lucas wrapped his arms around her, holding her tightly as her entire body shook. If the amount of tears she wept held any relation to the depth of her pain, then the fact that she was still alive was a fucking miracle. If it was too soon for her to say the words out loud and relive those nightmares, then he would wait until she was ready.

Burying his face in her hair, Lucas breathed her in, the scent of lavender and honey filling his lungs. He lost track of time as he held her, neither one of them ready to let go of the other. Finally, her tears stopped, and she pulled away to wipe her face on the sleeves of her sweatshirt.

When she met his gaze again, her lashes were spiked from her tears and her eyes practically glowed. Her face was blotchy and red, but she couldn't have looked more beautiful. She was here. She was his.

"I love you, Skye." Lucas tilted her head up and pressed his lips to hers, a gentle caress promising to make up for all the horrors she'd suffered at the hands of their enemy.

"I love you, too," she whispered when he pulled away.

"Now," Lucas said, releasing her, "tell me how you got here."

Skye batted the order away. "How about I tell you how we're going to get you out?"

Hope flared to life in his chest, and Lucas grinned. "Seriously?"

Skye nodded.

"Hell yes!" Lifting her, Lucas spun her in a circle before setting her back down. "I've been trying—and failing—to get out of this hellhole for what feels like forever."

"It requires a sacrifice, well, a soul sacrifice." She pulled a small piece of paper from her back pocket and handed it to him.

Lucas unfolded it and read the words she'd just said to him scrawled in her familiar handwriting. They still didn't make sense.

"Can I come back in?"

"Yes, Nan, of course," Lucas answered with a grin. Having two women he'd never thought he'd see again standing before him somehow made the Wasteland a bit more tolerable.

Glancing back at the paper, Lucas asked, "So, what's a soul sacrifice?"

"It doesn't have to be an entire soul," his Nan responded, as if that answered his question.

"What do you mean?" Skye asked.

"Oliver sacrificed a piece of himself—his magic, to be precise—in order to return home."

"But he still had power. If he sacrificed his magic in

order to leave, how did he have it when he returned?" Skye asked, her brows scrunched in confusion.

"He only sacrificed a part of his power. Ye see, the Wasteland only steals that which a Druid will not willingly give. It feeds off power; 'tis why Druids are trapped here. Most of them are too power hungry to want a life without all of their magic. When they will not give the Wasteland a portion of their power, it claims all of it until they fade away."

"So, that's why they all go crazy," Skye murmured.

His Nan nodded and moved toward the wall of runes. She ran her hand over the wall, pressing her palm against the stone right beside the largest rune. "I see ye tried to reactivate this."

Lucas shrugged. "I had to try something."

"This place requires a steep toll to enter or leave."

Lucas turned his attention to Skye, eyes narrowed. "So, without power to give, how did you get here?"

Skye looked away.

"I told ye, she sacrificed herself."

"Skye?"

She looked back up at him, her chin tilted defiantly. "I traded my life to get you out."

"You did *what*?" He couldn't help it, he shouted the question at her, terrified and distraught that she'd paid such a high price for his freedom. It wasn't worth it; nothing was worth Skye's life. Not even his own.

Skye straightened, not about to be bullied by him on this point. "Lizzie and James need you, Lucas. It will only be a matter of time before the Druid returns to take them out. You are the only one who can stop him."

"There had to be another way."

"There wasn't."

"Skye—"

"She's right, Lucas. In order for someone non-magical to get here, it takes a life. That sort of sacrifice has its own kind of magic. It must be something about that special kind of selfless love…" She trailed off, lost in thought, then, with a shrug, she added, "Anyway, 'tis why I sacrificed mine to send your Pop here. My love for my family was stronger than any ounce of self-preservation."

"So, what? I'm supposed to go back without you? I can't do that, Skye. I won't live without you. Losing you once almost destroyed me. I won't survive it a second time."

Skye blinked back fresh tears. "You have to. Lizzie needs you, Lucas. She's the last MacConnell standing, and she needs her brother."

"I won't settle for you not being around." He looked to his Nan. "You're both alive here, can you not come back with me?"

"I'm not sure. It's not something Oliver was willing to try," she responded dryly. "I suppose it could be possible, but it's just as possible that we're only alive here, fueled by the Wasteland's magic, and the second we go back to the real world, we'll be dead as doornails."

"I see where Lucas and Lizzie get their sense of humor," Skye said dryly.

"No reason to be down about it; we both willingly made the choice. Now, we must face the consequences."

"No," Lucas said forcefully, a muscle twitching in his jaw.

A life without Skye in it wasn't one he was interested in living. He would rather stay with her here, in the Wasteland, than go back without her. Shit, maybe he could send himself back here once he took care of the Druid once and for all. Anything would be better than having to spend the rest of his days without her.

"We should at least try to get you both back."

"I'm willing to try," Skye answered eagerly. "Even if it means dying all over again."

Lucas pulled her against him, desperate to hold her in his arms even if they weren't alone. He never wanted to stop touching her, especially if this was going to be one of his last chances to do so. What if she disappeared? What if he couldn't get back to her? There were entirely too many 'what ifs' for him to waste the opportunity to hold her.

Pulling back, he looked into her familiar eyes. Brushing a strand of hair from her forehead, he sighed. "Okay, Giovanni, how the hell do we get out of this place?"

CHAPTER 24

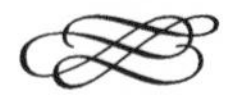

SKYE

Lucas and Maggie's heads were bent toward each other as they chatted about the best way for Lucas to make his offering to the Wasteland. A little bit of blood wouldn't do this time—he had to find a way to tap into his power and give just enough that the Wasteland would be satisfied, without weakening himself completely.

Luckily for Lucas, since he was one of only two remaining Druids, he had a considerable amount of power at his disposal.

A small smile played about her lips as she watched Lucas reconnect with his grandmother. There was an ease about his smile that she hadn't seen since they'd first gotten to know each other. Despite everything, Lucas had managed to find a small bit of happiness, and it made her heart soar.

He glanced over at her, and his smile widened. Every minute or so, he had a tendency to do that, as if he feared she'd somehow vanished while he wasn't looking. Skye couldn't blame him, she was guilty of that very thing.

Without warning, a sharp tingling built at the base of her neck. Skye let out a soft gasp and felt her knees give out beneath her. She was only partially aware of what was happening to her body as her vision pulled her under.

She didn't even have time to call Lucas' name before she was sucked in completely.

~

Skye looked around the cavern in confusion. She was standing farther back, but it was clearly the same cave she'd just been standing in. Maggie was drawing a rune on the ground, while Lucas tied a torn piece of cloth around his hand.

"Are you sure about this?" he asked, glancing to his left.

A second Skye, the one that existed in that moment, moved into view. "Yes, I'm sure."

"But I haven't been able to access my magic here—"

"Yes, you have. The Wasteland has been tricking you into believing otherwise. It's been siphoning the power you call up, keeping your spells from working as it steals your magic for itself."

Lucas grumbled, and she grinned before continuing, "This time, you are not trying to use your power, you are offering it. That's the difference."

With a sigh, Lucas brushed a kiss to her cheek and moved into the rune Maggie just completed.

"Ready?" Lucas asked.

Maggie and Skye nodded, each taking a place on the large circular rune. Lucas stood at the top, but inside the circle, while Maggie and Skye stood opposite, creating the base of a triangle.

The real Skye's stomach clenched with fear. If this was the future, which one of them was going to die? Was she about to find out what would happen to her and Maggie once Lucas left?

"It's going to work," Lucas said, holding out a hand for Skye to take.

She nodded, but Lucas must not have believed her. He closed the distance between them and kissed her hard and fierce. Maggie pointedly looked away, but she was smiling.

Just watching the kiss lit a fire within her, and Skye ached to be the one on the receiving end. If this was the future, it was definitely something to look forward to.

A discrete cough had the two lovers breaking apart with guilty grins.

"Alright, I'll see you on the other side."

Closing his eyes, Lucas tipped his head back and murmured, "Source and seed I offer, so that it may be planted anew and grow. Take this gift, freely given."

Light flared below their feet before Lucas had finished speaking. The light, a bright flickering green, danced beneath them, painting them in its glow. Lucas was illuminated by the same light, although it was coming from within, making him shine with its intensity.

His power, *Skye realized.*

Soon, the light was blinding, and even squinting, Skye could hardly see the three figures standing in the rune. It wasn't long, maybe three or four heartbeats later, when Lucas began to dim, and the flickers of light beneath their feet sank back into the ground. By the time the light faded completely, the three figures were gone.

Still within the vision, Skye looked at the empty circle and grinned. It had worked, and no one died.

A happy giggle escaped as the scene began to fade. Seeing what she needed, Skye was being pulled back to the present.

No one died, and still, she Saw the future.

The curse was broken.

"Skye! Skye, baby, answer me!"

A frantic Lucas was cradling her in his arms when her eyes opened.

"Man, those still suck," she croaked, licking her lips.

Skin pale and eyes wide with fear, he asked, "Who died?"

Skye shook her head, her grin so huge her cheeks hurt. "No one."

"What do you mean? That was a vision, wasn't it?"

Skye nodded, accepting his help as he lifted her to her feet.

"Then…I thought…how?" he asked, his brows furrowed.

"The curse…we broke it."

Mouth gaping, it took a second for the words to sink in and understanding to follow. "I'd forgotten all about that."

"What curse?" Maggie asked, concern darkening her eyes.

Holding hands, Lucas and Skye turned to face her.

"Our ancestors knew each other. Two of them were lovers once, but the Druid felt that the Gypsy had selfishly withheld information from a vision to hurt him. He cursed her and all of those that came from her line, to see only visions of death and be helpless to stop them."

Maggie gasped. "How terrible."

"Tell me about it," Skye said dryly.

Lucas chuckled. "In turn, the Gypsy cursed the Druid and those in his line, to never again know true love."

"So, how did ye manage to break it?" Maggie asked, wonder making her voice a bit breathless.

Looking at Skye, Lucas lifted their linked hands and pressed his lips to the back of her hand. "True love, obviously."

Delicious heat rolled through her, and Skye grinned. "Selfless love, actually. But yes, right idea."

He shrugged. "Same difference."

Skye laughed, joy making her giddy. Somehow, not even death had kept them from each other. What they had was strong enough to transcend death, and shatter the curse that spent lifetimes haunting their ancestors.

A weight she hadn't realized she was still holding onto dropped away, and Skye beamed. She and Lucas had found a new source of power, one forged in their love for each other. If they could overcome death, then the Druid didn't stand a chance.

Lucas ran a finger along her cheek. "That smile for me, Giovanni?" he asked, his eyes crinkling as he smiled down at her.

Her heart fluttered at the tender use of her name. "Lucas, we're going to win."

Eyes shining with excitement, he asked, "Is that what you Saw?"

"No, but I don't need to. I can feel it."

Still smiling, Lucas squeezed her hand. "So can I."

"So, what did ye See, lass?"

"How we're getting out of here."

"Thank fuck," Lucas breathed. "What do I need to do?"

With a laugh, Skye told them, and they got to work. For the first time, Skye wasn't afraid about one of her visions coming true.

CHAPTER 25

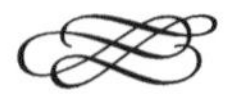

LIZZIE

Lizzie stood frozen, staring at the pool of dried blood where Skye had died. She squeezed her eyes shut against the onslaught of memories as a tear slipped down her cheek. Nearly a week had passed since her friend took her own life, but it could have been mere hours ago, judging by the gut-wrenching pain where her heart was supposed to be.

A week without Skye and without a single word from Lucas. There was no telling whether he'd found Skye or if her sacrifice had been in vain.

What in the hell were they supposed to do if Lucas never returned? She had a feeling waving a little white flag when the Druid came for them wouldn't keep him from ripping their throats out, if that's what he wanted.

"Hey." James pressed a hand to her lower back and dipped down to kiss the top of her head.

Lizzie looked up at him with an empty smile. His eyes were dark, his face slightly sunken in with the lack of sleep or proper sustenance. For the first time in as long as she could remember, she had no motivation to cook—or do anything, for that matter.

"Everything okay?" Lizzie asked, turning away from the stained carpet James avoided at all costs.

Watching Skye stab herself weighed on him. Lizzie knew on some level he'd believed he should have saved her, but you couldn't save someone who didn't want to be saved. Skye hadn't wanted to live in a world without Lucas, so she'd paid the ultimate price to bring him back. Shit, Lizzie couldn't blame her; she'd probably have done the same if it was James' life on the line, and very nearly considered doing it for Lucas—if she hadn't been terrified he'd find some way to bring her back just to kill her again.

"I haven't found anything. Giles just left for the day, said he'll bring over some more books in the morning."

Lizzie nodded but didn't respond.

They'd all been working nonstop to try and find another way into the Wasteland since Skye's death. The original plan had been for Giles to make the sacrifice that would send Skye through to reach Lucas, and when Skye flipped the script, they'd all been shocked that her body disappeared with the blinding light. Maybe it was because she was the only one standing on the rune, but that was mere speculation. It wasn't like they had a whole lot of prior knowledge to work with on how things were supposed to play out. Just Skye's and Giles' recounting of what happened the last time. Without knowing what became of Skye's body once—if—she reached the other side, all they could do was scramble to come up with a Plan B to get Lucas out.

"What do you want for dinner?"

"We can head into town and grab something at the pub?" James' eyes were hopeful.

Lizzie nodded. Getting some fresh air might do them both some good. "Let's do it. Fish and chips sound fantastic."

James smiled and kissed her softly. "I agree. I'll leave a note just in case."

It made her heart soar that he thought about that, too. Leaving a note would ensure that if somehow Lucas made it back before they did, he would know where to find them.

"I'm going to grab a quick shower and change out of these clothes."

"I think you look and smell wonderful already."

Lizzie glanced down at the sweats and oversized T-shirt she wore. *Wonderful, my ass.* She looked like she'd been sleeping in a gutter for the past week.

"I appreciate that, but I definitely need a shower." Lizzie reached up and gave him a loud smacking kiss on the cheek before heading toward the bedroom they shared.

After laying out a pair of jeans and a cream-colored sweater, Lizzie turned the hot water on and stepped beneath the spray. The warmth of the water, mixed with her lavender-scented body wash, calmed her, and for the first time since Skye's death, she felt alive. Not just a robot going through the motions, but a living, breathing, fully functioning human.

It was a nice feeling.

A few minutes later, Lizzie was stepping out of the shower and pulling on her sweater. After applying some mascara and lip gloss, she was ready for a night out with the man she loved. Taking a couple hours to forget about their current predicament was just what they needed. Hopefully, the break would have the added benefit of helping them see things with fresh eyes tomorrow.

"I feel so much better," Lizzie said a little while later, walking into the kitchen, where James stood drinking a small glass of scotch.

He'd changed, too, swapping the black sweatshirt for an olive-green button-up that complimented the hazel of his eyes perfectly.

"You look beautiful."

She raised an eyebrow. "I thought you said I looked good before?"

"You di—"

James was cut off by a large *thud* paired with the sound of shattering glass.

"Lucas?" Lizzie called out hopefully, rushing toward the noise.

"Lizzie, wait!" James shouted, gripping her arm and pulling her back before she could run out of the room.

"No, Lizzie, don't wait! Come on out and give Pop a hug!"

Lizzie froze as ice filled her veins. *So much for Lucas' protection runes.* Time seemed to stop as her brain struggled to process what was happening. The Druid was here, and they had no backup. They were completely and utterly fucked.

James held his finger up to his lips, asking her to be silent. She nodded, terror making speech impossible anyway. James threaded his fingers through hers. He gestured to the door leading outside from the kitchen, and she nodded again.

Heart in her throat, Lizzie followed James as they crept toward the door, careful to remain as quiet as possible. Reaching it, James started to pull it open. Lizzie flinched as the door creaked, and James shot her a wide-eyed stare, waiting a beat before pulling the door open further. Door open, James straightened slightly, but before he could make use of it, it slammed shut and the lock clicked.

"I just got here; I can't have you two leaving just yet."

As one, they turned to face him. Dread pooled in Lizzie's belly as she took in the crazed smile on the Druid's face. He was completely unhinged, his black eyes flickering with some kind of red light.

"The fun's just getting started."

James shoved Lizzie behind him. "What the hell do you want? Skye and Lucas are already gone."

"I figured that stupid Seer was going to try and go after him." He shrugged. "It's a shame to lose such a delicious toy, but I think we'll find a way to have fun without her. I'm nothing if not creative."

"You son of a bitch!" Lizzie screamed, launching herself at the robed figure.

James stopped her with a strong arm around her belly.

"That's not a very nice thing to say to your Pop now, is it, Lizzie-bear?"

Tears burned in her eyes at the old nickname. "Don't you dare call me that," she shouted. "You lost that right, you murdering bastard!"

"Ah, so you do have some spine after all! I was worried you'd inherited your Nan's weakness."

"You have no right," she growled, balling her fists as angry tears streamed down her face.

With the flick of his wrist, the Druid sent James flying across the room. James slammed into the living room wall before crumpling to the ground, unmoving.

"James!" Lizzie screamed.

"Oops, I guess that was a bit harder than I'd meant." The Druid shrugged. "One down, one to go." He moved toward her, and Lizzie shut her eyes, turning her face away.

"No! Please don't," she begged.

"Your pleas are worthless, Granddaughter." His hand closed around her throat, turning her head so she was forced to look at him. The heat of his breath washed over her face as he whispered, "Open your eyes."

The words made her shudder, but Lizzie did as she was told. Smiling, the Druid squeezed harder. She coughed, the additional pressure causing stars to explode in her eyes. She clawed at his hands, attempting to pry them from her neck, but nothing happened.

Bright green light filled the room, further blinding her. The Druid was ripped away from her, and Lizzie fell to the ground, gasping for breath.

"Lizzie! Are you okay?" Skye slid to her knees in front of her.

Lizzie stared up at her, dumbfounded. "Skye? Did-did I die, too?"

Skye gave her a small smile and shook her head. "No, sweetie."

"Then how?"

Glancing over her shoulder, Skye said, "Explanations are going to have to wait."

Following her gaze, Lizzie gave a dazed nod, staggering to her feet. *I'm seeing things. My brain was without oxygen for so long it caused permanent brain damage and now I see dead people.*

Stunned, Lizzie clutched Skye's arm, allowing herself to be pulled back into the center of the living room. Blinking, and pinching herself for good measure, Lizzie stared at her brother, who stood beside an older woman.

When the figures didn't budge, Lizzie sobbed, "N-nan?"

The woman turned around, and a radiant smile bloomed across her face. "Lizzie-bear, I can't tell ye how happy I am to see ya…all grown up."

Interrupting the tearful reunion, Lucas snarled, "Get up, you son of a bitch."

Realizing they weren't in the clear yet, Lizzie watched as the Druid pushed himself into a sitting position, his unblinking gaze never leaving her Nan.

"How are you here, Maggie?" the Druid demanded.

Scowling with disdain, she snapped, "Wouldn't ye love to know?"

"Don't you fucking look at her, asshole. I told you to get the fuck up!" Lucas shouted. A bolt of light shot from his hand, and the Druid flew up the wall, slamming into the ceiling. Plaster rained down on top of him as he hit the ground again.

Lucas hadn't so much as uttered an activation word to cast the spell. Lizzie swallowed. What the hell had happened to him while he was gone?

The Druid cast one last wide-eyed look at Maggie, then vanished.

"Fuck!" Lucas shouted, still primed for a fight.

Danger gone, Lizzie could care less that the Druid got away. All that mattered was that her big brother was here, and he was alive.

"Lucas!" Lizzie screamed, all but tackling him in her haste to reach him.

Eyes softening as he looked at her, Lucas wrapped his arms around her, hugging her tight. "I missed you, Lizzie."

Sniffling, she murmured, "I missed you, too, dumb-ass." Wiping her tears on the back of her hand, she pulled away and smacked him on the arm. "I told you your plan wouldn't work!"

"We're all here, aren't we?"

Eyes scanning the room, Lizzie nodded her agreement.

James groaned, and her eyes widened.

Moving away from her brother, Lizzie knelt beside her boyfriend, who was just sitting up, dazed. He bled from a small cut just above his eyebrow, but for the most part, he looked okay. "Are you alright?"

"What the hell did I miss?" he asked.

A teary laugh bubbled up, and Lizzie threw her arms around him. "I'm so glad you're okay."

"You and me both," he muttered, returning her embrace. Pulling back slightly, he took in the others standing nearby, watching them with amused smiles. "How hard did I hit my head?"

Brows furrowing with concern, Lizzie brushed her fingers along his scalp. "It doesn't look too bad."

"Then why can I see ghosts?" he asked.

Understanding dawned, and Lizzie threw back her head and laughed. "Those aren't ghosts, baby."

"Sorry, Matthews, you can't get rid of me that easily."

A grin stretched across James' face as Lizzie helped him stand.

"Fuckin' eh, man. I can't tell you how good it is to see you." James pulled Lucas into a one-armed hug, thumping him on the back a few times. "And you," he said, rounding on Skye, "don't you ever pull some shit like that again. You damn near gave me a heart attack."

Without waiting for a reply, he pulled her into his arms and hugged her. Lizzie thought she heard Skye mumble something, but it was impossible to know for sure. Pulling away from her, James glanced around the room. "So, who wants to fill me in?"

Smiling, heart full to bursting with joy that so many cherished faces—some she never thought she'd see again—were once again all in one room, Lizzie said, "I'll grab the scotch."

CHAPTER 26

LUCAS

"So, you just gave up a piece of your power?" Lizzie asked, her screech hitting a decibel only dogs should be able to hear.

Lucas winced and pointedly rubbed a finger in his ear. Lizzie just crossed her arms, waiting for his explanation.

"What else was I supposed to do, Lizzie? Hang out in the Wasteland until it claimed me, too?"

Frowning, Lizzie looked away. "No, I guess not. It's just, how are we supposed to beat the Druid now? Doesn't he technically overpower you?"

That really was the elephant in the room. What had seemed an obvious decision at the time, could very well turn around and bite him in the ass. Druids shared the same pool of power, so if Lucas gave up some of his portion, did that effect both of them, or just him? Based on the fear of his predecessors to make the offering to the Wasteland, he was pretty certain it was the latter.

He rubbed his neck, grateful he'd taken the time to heal his broken hand when they'd returned. "I don't feel any different." Although, that wasn't entirely true. His power was no longer an angry buzz beneath his skin, more like a pleasant hum. He could feel the weight of the others' stares as they watched him.

"And you cast that spell without a rune or anything," Lizzie murmured.

"What spell?" Lucas frowned.

"When you threw him into the ceiling?" Lizzie cocked an eyebrow as she motioned toward the plaster scattered all over the floor.

"I did?" Lucas asked, startled.

Lizzie's emphatic nod did little to reassure him. He would have sworn he'd shouted the word of power before slamming the Druid into the ceiling, but everything happened so fast, it was hard to recall each individual detail. He sincerely hoped his grasp on reality wasn't permanently altered by his trip to the Wasteland.

"Ye carry a vast amount of power, Lucas. What ye lost is but a drop in the bucket," his Nan said from her seat beside him.

Lizzie's eyes shone with uncontainable joy as she once again stared at their grandmother. She'd rarely glanced away from the silver-streaked blonde woman since they settled in to chat, apart from the times she was grilling him.

"Something I don't quite understand is why he sent you there in the first place," Matthews said. "Why not just kill you? He needed you dead in order for his plan to work, didn't he?"

"Apparently, he wanted to put me on ice," Lucas answered. He'd pieced that much together after the interaction in the warehouse. "Get everything else ready before taking me out."

"Seems like a lot of trouble to go through," Mathews said.

"Tis probable Lucas was becoming a bit of a thorn in his side," Nan said, turning her attention to Lucas, "and he'd hoped the Wasteland would drain ye enough that ye would be an easier target."

"That would explain why he was willing to tell us how to get Lucas out," Lizzie murmured thoughtfully. "He was already planning on doing it himself."

"Makes sense," Skye responded.

"How do you know so much about Druids, Nan?" Lizzie asked, no small amount of hero-worship coloring her voice.

Her husky laugh filled the room. "Well, it's hard not to the way yer Pop carried on about it in the beginning. He was always so proud of his heritage. It wasn't until Lucas came along that he really started to change. It must have been the first time he really felt the drain on his power."

Lizzie's face lost some of its glow as she glanced at her brother. "But why? If he was so proud of it, wouldn't he want to share it with someone?"

Their Nan shook her head, a sad smile on her face. "A normal man, maybe, but not Oliver. Realizing that more Druids in the family meant less power for him was something he did not handle well. He was a man possessed. The only thing that mattered in the end was his power."

"I wouldn't say the only thing," Skye piped up, walking back into the room with a fresh cup of steaming coffee.

Lucas chuckled as she poured a liberal amount of scotch into the cup. She winked at him before taking a sip and letting out an appreciative sigh.

"How do you figure?" Matthews asked, his hand running up and down Lizzie's arm.

"Well, I can't be the only one who saw how the Druid was staring at her," Skye answered, gesturing to Maggie.

Matthews nodded thoughtfully. "Yeah, but don't you just think that was the shock of seeing his wife alive again?"

"Maybe," Skye murmured. "But it felt like more than that to me. I mean…why else run off? The dude totally lost his mojo. He had the upper hand until we arrived, but once he saw Maggie, it was game over. He didn't even try to fight back."

"So, what, Nan's his kryptonite?" Lizzie asked with a laugh.

Skye shrugged. "All I'm saying is she makes him vulnerable. He's not immune to her like he is everything else."

Lucas looked over at his Nan, wondering what she thought about Skye's theory. "Nan?"

"Hmm?" she asked, blinking as he broke through her reverie.

"What do you think?"

She shrugged. "It's been a long time since I've seen yer Pop. Longer still since he was anything close to the man I fell in love with. I find it hard to believe that the sight of me would have any impact now."

"Well, if nothing else, you certainly caught him off guard," Matthews said.

Nan nodded. "True enough, but I wouldnae plan on it happening again."

The room fell silent except for the crackling of the fireplace.

"What are we going to do now?" Lizzie asked, looking around at the others.

As the one with the power, it was up to Lucas to offer the solution. "We hunt the bastard down."

"So soon? Are you ready to face him?" Skye asked, concern turning her eyes a deep bronze.

"We have to strike while we still have the advantage. For the first time ever, we have him on the run. We're not going to be in this position for long. We need to get to him before he has time to plan something."

"I agree. If he's running scared, it's the perfect time. Do you know where to find him?" Matthews asked.

"I found him once, I can do it again."

"I might be able to help with that," his Nan offered, her blue eyes twinkling at the idea of revenge. "I remember a few of his favorite hiding spots."

Lucas grinned at her. Who knew his grandmother would return from the dead and become their secret weapon? His hand snaked out and grasped hers, giving it a tight squeeze.

She returned it with one of her own, before pushing to her feet. "Ye'll have to excuse me. A few decades coated in sand has made taking a shower my first priority, and I think we could all do with a bit of a rest before rushing back out into danger."

The need to finish this once and for all pushed at him, but Lucas heard the wisdom in her words. There was no telling how things would play out, and if delaying the inevitable gave him one more night to hold Skye in his arms, he would hold onto that with every fiber of his being.

"Sounds good, Nan. We should probably include Giles in our planning anyway."

Her smile froze at the mention of the old Scot's name. There was history there, a complicated one from the looks of it. Recovering, she gave a nod, stopping on her way out of the room to press a kiss to Lizzie's head.

"Sleep well, children."

Lucas hadn't been a child for over twenty years, but he wasn't about to correct her. The fact that his Nan was here at all was a miracle. She could call him whatever she damn well pleased. The misty-eyed expression on Lizzie's face told him she felt the same.

"I still can't believe it," she whispered.

"I know."

"I hardly dared to believe you'd make it back, but to have all three of you…" Lizzie shook her head, her emotion making it hard for her to speak.

Lucas' eyes lifted to Skye. He knew exactly what she meant.

"C'mon, Lizzie. Let's head to bed and let these two have some time alone," Matthews murmured.

Lucas could have kissed his partner. Now that they were safe, and had a pocket of time to themselves, the only thing Lucas wanted to do was bury himself inside Skye.

"But they just got back." Lizzie pouted. "What if we go to sleep and they aren't here when we wake up?"

"We will be," Lucas assured her. "I promise, Lizzie."

silky strands of her hair back and over her shoulder, revealing the white square in its entirety.

Her breath hitched as he ran a finger along the edge of it, prying it loose as gently as possible.

"Did I hurt you?" he asked, going still as his eyes roamed over her face.

She jerked her head to the left but wouldn't meet his gaze.

"Skye?"

"I don't like thinking about it," she whispered. "At least when the bandage is covered by my hair, I can pretend that it never happened."

"What if you didn't need a bandage at all?"

That got her attention. Her eyes went to his, searching his face for the meaning of his words. "How?"

"Kicking ass and bleeding all over the place isn't the only thing I can do, ya know."

Her lips quirked up in the ghost of a smile.

Brushing his thumb along the line of her jaw, he added, "I was able to heal myself; it stands to reason I should be able to do the same for you."

"Do you really think you can do that?"

He shrugged. "Won't know until we try. But Skye?"

"Yeah?"

"Even if I can't, a few scars will never change how I feel about you, or what I see when I look at you."

"A few scars?" she scoffed. "Lucas, the asshole cut off my ear and fucking branded me with his evil runes."

Lucas pushed the hot rush of anger back down, burying it deep. There'd be time to call on it later, a time to repay

She still looked uncertain, but didn't resist when Matthews took her by the hand and led her from the room.

"We'll see you guys in the morning," his partner called.

Lucas nodded, hoping his appreciation for his friend's interference was communicated through the gesture.

"And then there were two," he said with a smile.

Skye grinned at him over the top of her coffee mug. "You heard your Nan, it's bedtime, Detective."

"Oh, I'm all about taking you to bed, Giovanni, but I have no intention of sleeping."

Her cheeks flushed a rosy pink. "Is that so?"

Standing, Lucas didn't break eye contact as he closed the distance between them. "You really going to fight me on this?"

"Nope," she whispered, looking up at him from beneath her lashes.

Tipping her chin up, he brushed his lips against hers in the barest hint of a kiss. Pulling back, he murmured, "Good."

A hint of white caught his eye, and Lucas shifted his gaze from Skye's parted lips to the bandage that peeked out from behind her braid. Her flush went from pink to crimson as she rushed to pull her hair back over the scrap of gauze.

He noted the change in her body, which was now curling in on itself defensively. *Hmm. Perhaps tonight would be about healing, rather than seduction.*

"Lucas," she protested as he grabbed the end of her braid and began to unravel it. Once loose, he brushed the each wound in kind, but there was no place for anger here. Only love.

"You're still the most beautiful woman I've ever seen," he declared, never once looking away from her.

Skye shook her head, a rush of emotions playing in her eyes. Looking conflicted, she asked, "How can you say that? You haven't even seen the worst of it."

"Then show me."

She glanced around the living room. "Here?"

"We're alone."

"Yeah, for now maybe…"

"Skye."

She looked up at him, her brows low over worried eyes.

"There's nothing you can show me that's going to change a damn thing between us."

Biting her lip, she nodded slowly, her hands already lifting to the side of her head to remove her bandage.

Lucas fought to keep his face impassive as he took in the angry red and black scar. The Druid must have done something to speed up the healing, because the wound was far less raw than he'd imagined, but it was gruesome all the same. He could feel Skye watching him and didn't want her to misinterpret his anger for disgust.

When he didn't say anything, she reached for the bottom of her sweater, sucking in a shaky breath before pulling it up and over her head in one quick move. Lucas' eyes dropped to her chest, letting out a hiss as he saw the first of the scars.

The biggest was a misshapen rune carved into her side,

its raised edges jagged and a red so deep it was almost purple. But the angry scar that hit him like a physical blow was the jagged line that disappeared into the middle of her bra. The one she'd gotten when she thought she'd died to save him.

Each of the scars she now carried were because of him, and Lucas had never been more aware that he in no way deserved Skye. In fact, he'd never felt more unworthy of someone in his entire life.

Lucas dropped to his knees in front of her, burying his face in her lap so she couldn't see the sheen of tears in his eyes.

"Lucas?" she asked, barely masking the fear in her voice as she ran trembling fingers through his hair.

"I'm going to kill him, Giovanni. I swear to you on my parents' graves that his time left on this earth is fucking limited."

"I know you will, Lucas."

"I'm just so fucking sorry."

"Lucas, no. Shh."

Skye was trying to tug him up, but Lucas wasn't fully in control of his emotions just yet, so he wrapped his arms around her hips and held on tight.

"This is my fault," he said, his words muffled into her lap. "None of this should have touched you. None of it would have if I'd just left you alone on that damn balcony like you wanted me to."

"Lucas, you had no more control over what's between us than you do the number of stars in the sky. I would suffer through everything, every terrible thing, again," she insisted, her voice husky with unshed tears, "because it ended up here, with me loving you."

"Skye," he groaned, pushing up to catch her lips with his.

"I mean it, Lucas," she said, pulling away to look in his eyes. "Curse or no curse. I was a ghost of a person before you slammed into my orbit and knocked me off course. I had my art, sure, but no friends, no real relationships. That's not a life, Lucas. I kept everyone at a distance after my grandmother died, too afraid of what attachment could lead to. Too afraid to really live, because I knew I'd eventually lose everyone I ever came to care about. Until you. Because of you, Lucas, I'm not that person anymore. You systematically destroyed every single excuse I ever clung to, like a fucking supernova"—she gave a watery chuckle—"you might have killed the girl I used to be, but never has there been anything more wonderful than being loved by you."

Lucas closed his eyes, no longer able to keep the first tear from rolling down his cheek. After everything she'd been through, she'd knowingly choose to do it all over again to be with him. Her honesty cut through him, laying his soul bare to hers. He didn't have the words to tell her what her confession meant to him, what hearing the words had done to him.

Swallowing a wave of emotion, Lucas did the only thing he could. Bending slightly, he scooped her up, cradling her to his body. Using instinct to guide his actions, Lucas drew on his power. It was slower to respond than it had been before, but the familiar tingling soon grew to a burn. Wiping a finger through each of their tears, Lucas drew the first rune over her heart, where the freshest scar laid. Then a second, over the

Druid's mark. And finally, a third, over the remains of her ear.

He didn't know if he said the word aloud or not, but when he opened his eyes, the scars were gone, and Skye glowed with the remnants of his power.

"You know the best thing about a supernova?" he asked in a rough voice as he started to carry her down the hall.

"What's that?" she whispered.

"There's nothing in any universe more beautiful than watching them shine."

CHAPTER 27

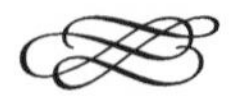

SKYE

Shutting the door behind them, Lucas slid her down his hard body before crushing his mouth to hers. Anticipation flooded her system, sending goosebumps flaring on her skin, and heat pooling between her legs.

He tasted of the scotch he'd had that evening, and Skye moaned as Lucas reached back and buried his hands in her hair. His hardness pressed against her, and Skye arched into it, desperate for the moment when the fabric barriers between them would be gone.

"You are so fucking wonderful, Skye," he whispered, trailing his lips down her neck.

The scruffiness of his beard scraped deliciously against her skin, and she arched back, giving him more access. He continued the tease down to her breasts, and with nimble fingers, he reached back and unclasped her bra. Lucas took a taut nipple into his mouth, and Skye groaned, arching back as his tongue traced circles around the delicate skin.

"Please, Lucas," she moaned.

He chuckled against her breast, and after pressing one last kiss, straightened to look down into her eyes. His own were laced with lust, and the passion reflecting in their depths only furthered her own desire.

"Not so fast, Giovanni. I have plans to savor every single delicious inch of you."

Lucas reached down and cupped her ass, lifting her as she wrapped her legs around his waist. The door pressed against her back as he took her mouth in another heated assault.

Dazed and aroused, Skye didn't realize he'd carried her to the bed until the mattress was at her back, and he was pulling away.

Lucas looked down at her like she was the most beautiful woman in the world, and it made her heart soar.

The mattress dipped with his weight, and he pressed a kiss to her stomach, just above the button of her jeans. Using one hand, Lucas undid the button and slid the zipper down slowly enough to drive a sane woman mad.

Skye arched up into him, craving the release that was already building inside despite the fact he'd barely touched her.

"Please, Lucas. I need you."

"Not like I need you, baby."

Sliding her jeans down, Lucas continued placing kisses down her legs, until he'd removed her pants and tossed them to the floor.

In an instant, Skye felt hot breath just over the black panties she wore. "Yes," she said breathlessly, burying her hands in the blankets beside her.

"That what you want?" He slid one finger beneath the

thin fabric, brushing over where she wanted him most, and Skye cried out.

"Yes, Lucas. Please."

He traced another finger against her skin, as he moved the fabric to the side and ran his tongue over her.

"You taste so fucking good."

Skye gripped the covers as Lucas drove her to the brink of insanity with each stroke of his tongue. Her body was on fire, flames lapping at every single inch of skin.

She cried out as the orgasm tore through her, but Lucas kept going, pulling every single moment of bliss from her before removing his clothes and covering her with his hard body.

He drove into her in one swift movement, and Skye wrapped her legs around his waist, urging him to move harder, faster, until his body released, and he collapsed on top of her.

Fire crackled in the hearth, shadows from the flames dancing on the walls around them. Skye reclined against Lucas, her head on his shoulder, tracing small circles on his smooth chest. Being here with him, spending the last few blissful hours making sweet love, had been more than she'd ever hoped to experience again.

Lucas pressed a kiss to her hair, and she looked up at him.

"Have I told you today how much I love you?"

Skye grinned. "A time or two."

"I love you, Skye."

"I love you, too, Detective."

Kissing her again, he sat up. "Should we talk about it?"

Skye adjusted so she could face him. "Talk about what?"

"How you were going to leave without telling me why?"

She sighed, having foolishly believed they'd already moved past it when they'd first talked about it back in the Wasteland. Too bad she couldn't simply forget the past few weeks of stumbling around in the dark.

"I told you I was sorry."

"I know you did, and I forgive you, but I want to make sure it's not something we ever have to deal with again. You have to trust me, trust me to do what I need to in order to keep you all safe."

"I do, Lucas. I promise."

Lucas smiled. "Good." He leaned back against the pillow and studied her. "Are you ready to talk about what happened to you?"

"Not particularly."

The thought of ever having to relive what she'd gone through, even if it was just conversation and not reality, wasn't something she wanted to do. Ever. The Druid still found her in her nightmares, where her subconscious forced her to relive the worst moments of her life. Skye knew they were just dreams, that she wasn't really being tortured, but they still felt like a violation.

Lucas' eyes darkened, the blue turning nearly cobalt as he picked up on all that she hadn't said. "I promise to spend the rest of my life trying to erase what he did to you."

All she could do was nod, her words buried somewhere deep inside where she was unable to reach. Skye hadn't told him about her hallucinations. About how the Druid visited her and said horrible things. Things that made her heart race with fear. How was she ever supposed to let go of what he did to her?

After a few heartbeats of silence, Skye cleared her throat and changed the subject, temporarily beating back her demons. "So, what's it like? Seeing your Nan again?"

"Unreal," he answered with a smile. "I can't believe she's alive, let alone sleeping in a room three doors down."

"It's amazing," Skye agreed. She still wasn't entirely sure how or why the Wasteland brought them back, but she wouldn't question the second chance she'd been given. "Think the plan will work? Using her to distract the Druid?"

"I'm not sure. I hope it will, at least long enough that I can kick his ass once and for all."

"Any idea how you're going to do that?"

Lucas shrugged. "I think better on my feet," he said, throwing her a wink.

Skye smiled, but fear of losing—of losing Lucas—nearly overwhelmed her. They were at the end of this war, and she knew deep down, the finale would be bloody. She could only hope the blood that spilled wasn't theirs.

CHAPTER 28

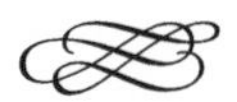

SKYE

Lucas was already gone by the time Skye woke up the next morning. She yawned and stretched, burying her face in his pillow and inhaling the scent of him. He was back. He was alive. Skye couldn't think of a better way to start the day.

Throwing on a pair of jeans and one of Lucas' T-shirts, Skye padded down the hall and into the kitchen, where the others were already deep in conversation. Lucas' eyes found hers as soon as she rounded the corner, but he didn't do more than offer her a smile before refocusing on his grandmother.

Maggie was busy unfolding a map, pointing at something as she smoothed it out on the kitchen table.

"Here," she said, tapping the spot.

Lizzie looked over her shoulder, trying to get a better look at whatever her Nan was pointing at.

"What is it?" James asked.

Knowing they'd fill her in on the important details, Skye poured herself a cup of coffee. She'd attended more than her fair share of these kinds of war meetings in the last handful of weeks. She didn't mind missing one if it meant she got to sleep in.

Leaning against the counter, Skye sipped on her go juice, only half listening to the others' murmuring until a knock sounded on the door.

"I'll get it," she called, waving the others back down. "You guys keep talking."

Opening the door, Skye gave Giles a confused grin. "Since when did you start knocking again?"

The Scot had taken care with his appearance that morning. He wore a pair of pressed tan trousers with a dark gray jacket that had black suede elbow patches. His button-up shirt was the same color as his eyes and mostly hidden beneath a brown and green plaid vest.

Smoothing down his hair, he smiled at her. "With the lady of the house returned, it didn't seem polite to barge in."

Understanding dawned on her. "You worried about seeing Maggie again, Giles?"

The tips of his ears went pink, and he cleared his throat. "Just being respectful is all."

"Right," Skye teased, pushing the door open wider. "Well, I'm hardly the lady of the house, but come on in." She winked as she stepped aside.

Giles crossed the threshold and then paused again, pivoting to face her. "'Tis good to see ya, lass."

"You too, Giles."

He stared at her, his moss-green eyes clouded with an emotion she didn't recognize. He gave her shoulder an awkward pat and then moved past her and into the kitchen. The others fell silent as Giles cleared his throat.

"Mornin'."

Skye was right behind him, so she could only see Maggie's expression as she spotted her old friend for the first time in almost three decades. Her smile was soft, her eyes filled with a silvery sheen.

"Giles, ye've hardly aged a day."

"Ye always were a pretty liar, Mags."

Pushing back from the table, Maggie stood and threw her arms around Giles' neck. "I'm so glad to see ya."

Giles' voice was gruff as he wrapped an arm around her waist and used the other to stroke her hair. "Not near as much as I, Mags. Not near."

The two clung to each other, and Skye forced herself to look away. This was a private moment, not one meant to be intruded on by shameless voyeurs.

"Oy, you lot. Back to your maps," Skye called.

Lizzie shot her a grin and looked back at the table, James following suit.

"Oy? Lot? Did we step back in time when we went through that portal?" Lucas teased.

Skye shrugged, sliding into the chair beside him. He wrapped his arm around the back of her seat, and Skye angled her body into his warmth. He brushed a kiss to her cheek and returned his attention to the map, filling her in on their plan.

"Nan says that Pop had a place he liked to go when he wanted to perform complex rituals." He pointed to a spot on the map. "It's a stone circle not too far from here."

The mention of a stone circle sent fear skittering

through her. *Everything has changed since your vision. That future isn't going to come true.* Still, it hit a bit too close to what sent her packing in the first place, and it was tricky keeping the note of panic out of her voice.

"And she thinks he'll be in hiding there?" Skye asked. A stone circle wasn't much of a hideout.

"Not quite."

"We're going to set a trap," Lizzie explained.

"With what bait?"

"Me," Maggie said, as she and Giles took the last two seats at the table.

Giles gave her a worried glance but didn't comment.

"I'm sorry," Skye said with a shake of her head, "I'm not following."

"Stone circles have always been linked to Druids' most sacred holidays and rituals. They are almost always built on top of intersecting ley lines," Maggie said.

"Because of the power boost," Skye said with a nod. "What's that got to do with you?"

"He has no clue what the Wasteland might have done to me, a mere mortal, after all that time. He's going to be intrigued, especially if there's a hint that I might hold some of its secrets."

"But you said that the Wasteland has no real effect on a mortal," Skye said, furrowing her brow.

"Right, we know that, but Oliver doesn't."

"So, you're thinking that if he finds out you're at his secret Druid place, it will lure him out of hiding?"

Maggie nodded. "He'll want to know why I'm there, if nothing else."

Scanning the table, Skye asked, "Is it just me, or does that seem too simple?"

"Oliver would have spelled the place to alert him if another Druid found it," Giles said.

"So, Lucas will trigger the alarm as soon as we get there," Skye replied.

"Right, but when the Druid arrives, he won't find Lucas, he'll find Nan," Lizzie added.

"Oh," Skye murmured, finally getting it. "So, he'll mistakenly think that Maggie has somehow inherited some of the Druid's power via the Wasteland."

"Exactly. If all goes well, he'll be too distracted by the idea to realize he's walking into our trap," Lucas said.

"Literally," Lizzie said with a grin.

Skye must have still looked confused because Lucas elaborated further. "We're going to rune the center of the stone circle so that when the Druid moves into the middle, he'll be trapped."

"A barrier rune?" she guessed.

"A Druid's snare," Maggie corrected.

Skye shook her head, not familiar with the term.

"It's like a cage," Lucas explained, "without a door or a key. Once he is stuck, he cannot get out, unless I will it. He will be, in a word, fucked."

"Alright, so he's locked up, then what?" Skye asked.

"Then I kill him," Lucas said, his eyes flickering with a hint of his power.

Somber eyes met hers around the room. Lucas was making it sound easy, but nothing about facing off with the Druid had ever been easy. Thus far, he'd beaten them every step of the way.

"And we really think this will work?" Skye asked.

"It's our best shot, Giovanni."

Skye looked at Lucas and sighed. "So, what are the rest of us supposed to do?"

Lucas opened his mouth to reply, and Skye cut him off by pointing a finger at him. "And don't you dare say stay here, because you know there's no way in hell that I'm letting you out of my sight for a second to face that bastard on your own."

His eyes were warm as he laced his fingers with hers. "No, I wouldn't ask you to stay behind. Not after everything he's put you through. This isn't just my fight anymore, it's all of ours."

Skye glanced around the table as Lucas received a nod from every member of their party. Every single one of them had been hurt by this bastard, one way or another. Everyone here held their own personal grudge against the Druid.

Clearing his throat, Giles said, "I have an idea."

He flinched as the others spun to look at him, but Maggie patted his arm encouragingly. He seemed to sit up straighter as he filled them in.

"There was a spell I found; it's an amplification spell."

"Like what the ley lines do?" James asked.

"Not quite," Giles said. "While we do not have power of our own, not like Lucas and Oliver do, we do have something we can offer to help him."

"A Druid's magic is said to be the essence of life itself," Maggie said softly, her eyes narrowing on Giles' face as he nodded.

"Right. So, for a limited span of time, a Druid could

amplify his own power by borrowing the life energy of another. Or in our case, others."

"Isn't that dangerous?" Lizzie asked.

"It could be, in the hands of one who wanted to harm. But in order to work, it must be gifted willingly, which is likely the only reason Oliver hasn't been doing it this whole time."

Lucas didn't look convinced. "How does it work?"

"We link ourselves to ye, so that when the time comes, ye can draw on our energy."

"Like a battery," James said.

Giles nodded. "Sure."

"Batteries can be drained." Lucas narrowed his eyes. "What's going to keep me from taking too much from you guys?"

Giles shrugged. "It's a risk. We'll have to trust ye to only take what is needed."

"Is there a way to limit what he can take?" Skye asked.

"Not that I know of."

"But if we do it as a group, doesn't that increase our chances of no one person being consumed?" James asked.

"That's the hope," Giles said.

"No." Lucas shook his head. "No way, it's too dangerous. I could lose control and kill you all."

"Lucas," Maggie said.

"I don't want to put anyone else at risk."

"You just said we're all in this," Skye murmured, squeezing his hand. "Let us help you."

"Ye need the power, Lucas. It's the only way to balance the scales."

His Nan's words did what the others could not. Hanging his head in defeat, Lucas muttered, "Fine."

"So, what do we need to do?" Lizzie asked.

"First, I'm going to need to take some blood from each of ye."

"Of fucking course you are," Lucas groaned. "Just once, I wish I didn't have to saw myself in half for shit to work."

The others chuckled at his heartfelt gripe.

"How much do you need this time, Giles? One vein or two?" Lucas asked, rolling up a sleeve.

Giles smiled. "It shouldn't take much, we just need enough that you can draw the rune on each of us."

"How big's the rune?" James asked, looking pale.

Lizzie pat his hand. "Not loving the idea of smearing blood on your body, babe?"

Skye watched his throat bob. *Poor guy.*

"It helps if you think of it as finger paint," Skye offered.

James nodded. "I'll try to remember that."

Lizzie grabbed a clean bowl from the dish rack behind her while Giles pulled out a small pocket knife from his pocket.

"You're like a damn boy scout, Giles. Always prepared," Lucas said dryly.

"A what?" Giles asked.

"Never mind."

Lizzie and James snickered.

"Does it matter who goes first?" Skye asked.

"Not who's first. Lucas must be last, though, since 'tis his blood that will bind them all together."

"Then let's get it over with," she said, holding out her arm.

"Wait," Maggie said, standing. "If we're going to do this, let's do it right."

She rushed out of the room, and the others glanced at each other in confusion. She was only gone for a few minutes before returning with a small red book, a chalice, and a silver knife.

"You didn't like our supplies?" Lizzie asked, looking at her chipped bowl with purple heather hand painted along the sides.

"When a Druid performs a ritual, he should use the proper tools. It adds intention and meaning to the words."

"And here I was thinking a finger in the palm of my bleeding hand was good enough," Lucas said.

His Nan grinned. "Oh, it will work in a pinch, but if I learned anything from Oliver, it was that serious magic should be treated as such."

Her words sobered the group, each one of them losing their smiles as they nodded. What they were doing was serious. This ritual could be the difference between all of them walking away from the fight alive, or zipped up in body bags.

"Alright, Nan, show me what to do," Lucas said, his blue eyes leveled on hers.

"Repeat after me." Sliding the blade along her palm, she said, "*Beannaich an tabhartas seo.*"

Lucas repeated her words, the Gaelic flowing from his lips as if it was his native language. In a way, Skye guessed that it was.

"*Air a sgaradh le neart an neach a tha a 'toirt*

seachad," Maggie prompted, as her blood dripped into the chalice.

"They don't expect us to be able to remember all that, do they?" James whispered loudly.

Skye grinned as Maggie shook her head, and Lucas repeated her words.

Passing the chalice to Giles, Maggie said, "*Is dòcha gun toir e buaidh."*

Once Lucas was finished, Lizzie asked, "Can you tell us what it means, Nan?"

She nodded, speaking the words in English as Giles made his offering, and Lucas spoke in Gaelic.

"Bless this offering. Infused with the strength of the giver, may it bring me victory."

The hair on the back of Skye's arms stood on end.

One after another, the remaining four added their blood to the chalice, each one of them saying, "May it bring us victory," before passing the items to the next in line.

Once the blood was collected, Lucas looked expectantly at his Nan. "What next?"

Flipping open the book, she spun it around to him. "Now ye draw that, but don't use the activation word until it's time."

"Where should I put it?" Lucas asked, studying the curling rune.

Maggie pulled down the neck of her blue sweater. "Just here, above our hearts. Spells are about symbols, Lucas. When it comes to the source of life, ye always use the heart."

Since she was sitting closest, Skye copied Maggie's move and tugged her shirt down.

"That's my favorite shirt, you know," Lucas said in a low voice, his lips lifting in a small smile.

"Is it?"

Dipping his finger into the cup of warm blood, he nodded. "It is now that I've seen you in it."

Skye rolled her eyes as he traced the rune onto her skin. As soon as he completed the last flourish, the rune shone a soft green and faded into her skin.

James let out a low whistle. "This wizard shit will never cease to amaze me."

Scowling, Maggie said, "They're called Druids, not wizards, lad."

Skye threw her head back and laughed, the sound rolling through the kitchen until the others joined in. They might be on the brink of their final battle, but they would live each moment they had left.

Together.

CHAPTER 29

LUCAS

Lucas stared at the patchy grass between the towering stone slabs of the circle. They'd had to walk most of the way here, and without even setting sight on the first of the stones, Lucas knew when they'd arrived. He could feel it in his blood, a tingling awareness that crawled up the back of his neck. It was invigorating, like he'd slammed back seven shots of espresso.

It rained most of the day, so the ground beneath them was a muddy mess, squelching loudly in protest every time he took a step, but the sky was clear now, and the first of the night's stars shone down on them.

"I don't like this place," Skye said, rubbing her arms as she stopped beside him.

"Really?" he asked, surprised. He could easily see himself coming back here after everything was over.

She eyed him. "Maybe it's my Gypsy sense of self-preservation."

Lucas grinned. "Must be."

"It's almost time," she whispered.

"I know."

"Are you ready?"

Her hair blew across her face in the breeze, and Lucas brushed it back. "As ready as I can be."

She turned her face into his caress, her eyes falling closed. "We should probably get into position then, we don't have much time before he gets here if Giles' estimates are correct."

Lucas nodded, linking his fingers through hers. "Let's do it, then."

He signaled to the others, and they met near the Easternmost stone. "It's showtime. You remember the signal, Nan?"

She nodded, her blue eyes shining. "However this ends, I am so proud of you, both of you," she said, reaching out to cup Lizzie's cheek.

"We're just glad to have you back, Nan." Lizzie covered the older woman's hand with her own.

"I cannae begin to tell ye how wonderful 'tis to see ye all grown up, lass. Ye have the look of yer mother. She wore her hair just the same," Nan added, touching Lizzie's trademark bun.

Lucas watched with a smile as Lizzie's eyes teared up, and she responded with a choked, "Thank you."

Turning her attention to him, Nan said, "I'm so grateful I had a chance to see the man ye've become, Lucas. So much like yer father."

"Me too, Nan." Lucas swallowed back the lump forming in his throat. His Nan's words sounded suspiciously like a goodbye, and he refused to accept the idea that they may lose tonight.

"All will be well, Mags." Giles stepped forward and smiled at her.

"Aye, I believe it will be."

They shared a look so chock-full of emotion, that Lucas forced himself to look away. It reminded him too much of the looks he and Skye'd shared when they found each other again.

Gripping Skye's hand, Lucas followed Lizzie and James out of the circle and toward the tree line just on the other side of the clearing. They needed to stay hidden long enough for the Druid to make his way into the center and right into their trap.

Once the bastard couldn't leave, Lucas would make his grand entrance, and then he'd end this thing once and for all.

"Are you scared?" Skye whispered once they were out of the clearing.

Lucas smiled down at her. He'd never admit it, but he was terrified. He'd set up stings like this before, but the outcome had never been so crucial, or so unpredictable. The Druid was no ordinary criminal, and no matter what Lucas told himself, the evil bastard wasn't going to make this easy. But now wasn't the time for him to admit that to the rest of them. The others looked to him as their leader. They took their cues from him, used his strength to bolster their own, and right now, they needed to see unflappable confidence. Anything else would lead to doubt and uncertainty, two things they could not afford. Unwavering belief, the lack of hesitation in the most critical moments, would be the difference in how this played out.

Lucas brushed a kiss to Skye's forehead. "Not even a little. I've got this, Giovanni."

Her lips tightened; she knew him well enough to sense he wasn't telling the full truth. Before she could dig further, Lucas pulled her against him for a soft, lingering kiss. If anything happened to him tonight, at least they'd been able to share these last few months together.

"Now, we wait," Giles said, taking his place beside Lucas.

Pulling back from Skye, Lucas confirmed, "Now, we wait."

Nan stood in the center of the clearing, the stone sentinels surrounding her like silent guards. Her hands were folded together as she stared straight ahead. She looked like she was preparing to deliver a speech and was just waiting for the audience to settle. There was no hint of fear about her. The woman was made of steel.

It wasn't long, maybe all of five minutes, before a blast of light shot through the night, just outside the circle of stones. His Nan didn't turn toward it, didn't so much as flinch or acknowledge it in any way. But Lucas did. He straightened as the Druid stepped from the portal—which had already started to fade—a leer stretching across his face at the sight of his wife.

"Seems rather foolish to venture out at night. All sorts of monsters could be lurking about."

It took everything in Lucas to not run out there now. Skye squeezed his hand, a silent reminder that he needed to wait.

"After years married to the worst of them, I find that monsters don't much frighten me anymore. Hello, Oliver."

Atta girl, Nan.

"Maggie." The Druid tilted his head and took another step toward the circle. "What brings you all the way out here?"

"I needed to see ye."

"Oh?"

Come on, you bastard, just a few more steps.

"Aye. Have some things to tell ye."

"Missed me, then?"

"Hardly."

Just a little closer. Lucas' fingers bit into the bark of the tree he hid behind. The Druid was nearly inside the stone circle now; it was only a matter of a few more steps, and then Lucas could make his move.

"Tell me, Maggie-girl, what did being trapped all those years do to you? Druid or no, part of me wondered if you would up and disappear just like the others."

One more step and he'd be right on the edge of their snare.

"Wouldn't ye like to know?"

"I would. I've been wondering if it was possible for anyone to leave the Wasteland unchanged, and it seems that they cannot. I could feel it as soon as you stepped foot in this place, you know. The power; a *Druid's* power." He took the final step, crooning, "Imagine my delight when it was you I found waiting for me."

With one last look at Skye, Lizzie, Matthews, and Giles, Lucas stepped out of the tree line. The Druid's black eyes landed on Lucas the second he was clear. Lucas smiled.

"'Och, I have no doubt ye felt the power, Oliver, but it was never mine."

Snarling, the Druid tried to take a step back but was thrown forward by the force of the barrier. Landing on his hands and knees, the Druid looked up. Lucas' smile grew at the sight of the old man's fear.

"Fools!" The Druid pushed himself upright and charged.

Lucas flung a hand up, sending him flying back and away from Maggie.

"It's over, Oliver. Ye will lose tonight, and I, for one, cannae wait to see ye bleed," Maggie sneered, stepping out of the circle.

Lucas exchanged a look with his Nan before taking her place inside the stones.

Getting to his feet, the Druid tried to brush the mud from his cloak, but only served to smear it in deeper. With a shake of his head, he looked toward Lucas. "Seems you do have a few tricks up your sleeve, Grandson."

Lucas continued moving, circling the Druid. "More than a few."

"You may have trapped me, but you will not win. I possess more power than you could ever begin to comprehend. Isn't that right, Seer?" he asked, throwing a grin at Skye, who stood just outside of the stones.

Skye went pale at the Druid's words. Even from here, Lucas could see her throat bob. He clenched his fist. *Focus*.

"Ah, look. She remembers our time together fondly. Don't worry, Seer. We'll be together again soon."

Lucas growled, and the Druid chuckled, throwing out a hand. Power slammed into Lucas' chest, but he held his ground. His feet slid in the mud, but he didn't fall, and the look of surprise on the Druid's face brought a smile to his own. As much as he wanted to draw out this bastard's suffering, it was more than time to end this.

Focusing on the words of power he'd seen scrawled in his Nan's book, Lucas repeated them over and over, *A'tighinn beò*. Without turning to them, he knew exactly where each of his friends stood. He could practically see them in his mind. The harder he focused on the words, the brighter they shone.

Still smiling, Lucas repeated the phrase a final time, drawing on the lives of those around him. Power flooded his system, and Lucas held his palm up, calling it forward. It was immediately responsive, threading through his body and collecting in his hands. The Druid stared in growing horror as the tiny needles of power gathered and began to pulse a deep red. Once the orb had grown to the size of a beach ball, Lucas released it straight into the Druid's chest.

The force of the power threw his enemy back against the barrier. He ricocheted off and slammed back into the ground. The Druid was on his feet in an instant, but Lucas was ready.

Power unlike anything he'd ever felt surged through Lucas' veins, and he grinned, immediately throwing another blast at the Druid, who stumbled back again before falling to his knees.

"Skye!" Lizzie's startled cry pulled his focus.

Lucas looked over just in time to see Skye stumble. *Did I use too much? Is she having another vision?*

He started toward her, but Nan shook her head as she and Lizzie helped Skye back to her feet. Skye's eyes fluttered open, looking huge in her pale face as they flared wide.

Lucas turned his attention back to the Druid a second too late. A blast of power barreled into him before he could block it. He slammed back into one of the large stones. Vision swimming and ears ringing, Lucas staggered, but didn't hit the ground.

"Your Nan believes family makes you stronger," the Druid sneered, moving closer. "But the only purpose they serve is to distract you." Black power blazing in his eyes, he gripped Lucas' throat.

Flashes of his past ran through Lucas' mind, and for a moment, it was as if he was standing back on that Chicago balcony with Skye for the first time. He could clearly see every second of that night, right down to the strands of hair blowing across her face in the chilly air.

He needed his future with her, needed to know what it would be like to grow old and share a love that would last a lifetime. That was where his power came from, his ability to love others rather than destroy them. Something the asshole in front of him would never understand.

If a Druid's power was tied to the essence of life itself, that meant it could only be strengthened by love.

Love is what gives life meaning.

No matter what this bastard thought, being surrounded by people you loved would always be a strength.

Still connected to the others, Lucas lightly tugged at

the strands of power, careful not to overdraw. Inhaling deeply, he opened his eyes.

"You're wrong," he choked out, slamming his palms into the Druid's chest.

The Druid flew back, landing in a heap several yards away. Lucas stalked toward him, his hand already wrapped around the hilt of the runed dagger tucked into his waistband when the man who'd once been his Pop rolled onto his back. Without hesitation, Lucas attacked, slamming the dagger down into the bastard's chest.

The Druid gasped, gurgling as bright red blood trickled from his mouth.

Lucas twisted the dagger, and the Druid gave a jolt beneath him before going limp.

"Have fun in hell, asshole," he murmured.

Just as he was about to stand, a wave of pure power washed over Lucas, knocking him off the Druid and into the mud. The world tilted and spun around him, one giant whirl of color, before everything went black.

CHAPTER 30

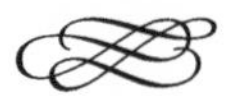

LUCAS

Lucas stood alone in the center of the stone circle; the others were nowhere to be found. Electric blue power swirled around him and the ancient stones, linking them in some kind of magical light show. Wind roared as the power pulsed and spun, making it nearly impossible to hear anything but his own thoughts. What the hell happened? Did he send me back to the Wasteland?

Without warning, the magic converged, turning into one single beam that shot toward him. Lucas fell to his knees as power surged into his veins. His body spasmed, eyes rolling back in his head as the shared consciousness of his entire Druid line poured into him through the solid stream of magic.

"Accept your inheritance," a multitude of voices whispered, surrounding him with the sound.

"Our power is now yours."

"Use it wisely."

So many voices layered over one another, making it impossible to single out any individual speaker.

Lucas screamed, pain ripping through him as his body was assaulted by magic—both the light and the dark—pouring into him and rearranging the very molecules of his body. Just as he was sure it was the end of him, the pain subsided, and the wind died down, leaving him gasping for breath on his hands and knees in the center of the circle.

"Feels good, doesn't it?"

Opening his eyes, Lucas scrambled to his feet as the soulless black gaze of his twin stared back at him. The emptiness of the stare shook him just like the first time he'd seen him, back when he absorbed the power hidden within the O'Leary journal.

His twin grinned, the smile entirely too reminiscent of the Druid for comfort. "I told you our power would make or destroy us."

"What the hell are you talking about? I'm fine."

His twin cocked his head to the side. "Are you?"

Lucas glanced down at his hands, which glowed with the magic running through his veins.

"All that power…imagine what you could do with it. The good or…" his twin trailed off, shrugging and still smiling that same half-demented smile.

Lucas didn't need him to finish his sentence to understand the implication. He could feel the truth of his twin's words radiating through him, the endless possibilities that came with ultimate power. All of the things he was capable of now…and there would be no one to stop him. He was the last of the Druids.

"You have to choose a path."

Lucas' gaze shot back to his twin. "And you're here to help me do that?"

"I'm here to remind you what's at stake."

In an instant, the clearing changed, and they were no longer alone. Where there had once been green grass, now only carnage. Everywhere he looked, the ground was coated in dark red blood, the bodies of those he loved strewn across the turf, slaughtered where they'd stood.

"No," Lucas gasped, stricken as his eyes landed on Lizzie's lifeless body. Her arm was flung out toward Matthews, as if she'd reached for him even in her final moments. And her eyes—normally so full of life—were frozen open in a horrified stare aimed directly at him.

"This is what awaits you if you choose the wrong path."

"No, I don't want this! What am I supposed to do? Tell me what to do!"

"There is more than one host for the MacConnell line. Times are changing." His twin began to fade, and Lucas rushed toward him.

"What the hell does that mean? I thought the Druid was dead?"

"You are the Druid now."

Lucas shook his head. "I'll never be like him."

"That's yet to be seen." His twin disappeared with a soft chuckle, and the world faded away.

~

"LUCAS!"

"Lucas, stop fucking around and wake the fuck up!"

Lucas blinked open his eyes. Skye and Lizzie's pale faces swam into view, their eyes wide as they looked down at him. Both women scrambled away as he sat up.

"Lucas?" Skye whispered softly.

So much power. I could do anything with this much magic at my disposal...

"Lucas, come back," his Nan called, taking a step toward him.

'You are the Druid now.' His twin's warning came back to him, and Lucas scooted away.

"Get away from me," he warned as dark thoughts continued to fill his mind: blood-soaked grass, his sister's sightless eyes. And then there were the voices.

'You don't need them.'

'They make you weak!'

"What can we do?" Lizzie asked, panic lacing her tone.

Lucas turned away. He couldn't risk looking at them. Not when a dark part of him wanted them gone—forever.

"'Tis too much power for him alone," Giles answered.

"Then tell us what to do!" Skye screamed.

Lucas could do nothing but stare at his hands as his new power lured him into the dark. Fighting for control, he replayed the words his twin had spoken. *'There is more than one host for the MacConnell line. Times are changing.'*

What the fuck did it mean?

"Snap the hell out of it, Lucas!" Lizzie raged at him, and Lucas' eyes flew open.

"Lizzie!"

She straightened, clearly stunned that her outburst had gotten through to him. "What?"

"I need you," he ground out as the voices filled his head once again.

"Do not waste your power."

"Use what is rightfully yours."

"Need me for what?" she asked, taking a hesitant step away from him.

He must've looked as nuts as he was starting to feel.

"Please," he pleaded.

She gave him a long stare but slowly began to walk toward him.

"I need the blade."

Matthews stepped forward and stopped Lizzie with a hand on her arm. "For what?" he asked, looking at Lucas.

"Stop fucking around!" Lucas roared. His time was running short, and he knew without a doubt what he had to do before he lost control completely.

"I'll be fine," Lizzie assured Matthews, before pulling the runed dagger from the Druid's chest.

Her movements were unhurried, casual even. Had Lucas not been on the verge of falling into the abyss of his power, it might have pissed him off. The truth was, in the state he was in, they should all be afraid of him. Hell, at the moment, he terrified even himself.

"Here," Lizzie said, handing him the blade.

After wiping it on his jeans, Lucas ran it across his palm. "Hand," he ordered.

Lizzie hesitated.

"Give me your fucking hand, Lizzie! Please," he added

when she jumped. "I don't know how much longer I can hang on."

Something in his eyes must have proved his words because Lizzie held her hand out, palm up, and Lucas sliced through the delicate flesh.

"Fuck, that hurts," Lizzie hissed.

Tossing the blade aside, Lucas gripped her hand with his injured one so their wounds touched, mixing his blood with hers. Staring at his sister, Lucas murmured the words that would forever change both their lives.

"*A roinnt mé mo chumhacht.*"

I share my power.

Lizzie's eyes blazed the same electric blue as the power that had swirled around Lucas in the circle. She gripped Lucas' hand hard as the excess power drained out of him, surging into her through their joined hands. As they held hands, more power flowed around them, cocooning them in a multitude of color as their heritage was shared.

Alone, the power was too much for him, but with Lizzie, they could each carry a portion of the burden. Two halves of the same whole.

"What's happening?" she called to him, terror lacing her voice.

"It's the only way," he yelled back.

'There is more than one host for the MacConnell line.'

After a moment, the vibrant colors encompassing them died down, and Lizzie stared back at him, understanding shining in her bright blue eyes. MacConnell eyes.

"What the hell just happened?" Matthews asked, rushing toward them. "We couldn't get to you!"

Lizzie smiled at Lucas, who finally felt more like himself. No more power-hungry, murder-everyone, rule-the-world thoughts filling his mind. For the first time since he'd killed the Druid, Lucas turned to Skye, whose lips were curled in a soft smile.

"The power was too much for him to handle alone," she explained.

His Nan gasped, covering her mouth with a hand. "Ye made Lizzie a Druid."

Lucas nodded, winking at his sister. "The first female Druid in history."

Lizzie beamed, staring down at her hands. "Fuck yes."

CHAPTER 31

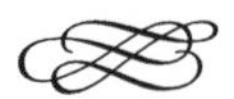

LIZZIE

Lying in bed, Lizzie stared down at her hands. How was it she could feel so different inside, and yet still look exactly the same on the outside?

It was as if the power Lucas transferred to her had burrowed its way down into her very soul and become just as much a part of her as any of her limbs. She could feel the life force of everyone and everything around her, strands she could examine and know she was never alone.

The world was brighter now, her power coating everything in a beautiful filter that amplified the colors.

Not to mention, having power was awesome as hell.

Seeing Lucas wake up with black eyes had certainly been amongst the scariest things she'd ever seen, but now that he was back to normal, she couldn't keep the smile from her face.

They'd won! They'd actually beaten the Druid bastard who'd tried to kill them multiple times, and who'd tortured one of her best friends. It was all behind them now. Finally, they could move on with rebuilding their lives. Eventually, they'd travel back to Chicago so she could rebuild her diner, and things could go back to the way they were.

Better even.

Now, she had James. Her eyes traveled over to the slightly ajar door to the bathroom, where he was showering. Their future would hold so many incredible things that had nothing to do with her newfound power, and everything to do with being together.

Glancing back at her hands, she sifted through the Gaelic words of power that she suddenly knew as if it had been her first language. The knowledge must have been transferred to her along with the power. Apparently, she was the next best thing to Google Translate…at least when it came to the English and Gaelic languages.

"*Solas*," she whispered. Her palm blazed with white light, and Lizzie smiled as she flexed her fingers, causing the orb to dance and cast its flickering shadows on the wall beside her.

For so much of her life, she'd been powerless. First with her ex, and then again when the Druid started tormenting them.

Now, she'd never be powerless again.

Not with half the MacConnell Druid power running through her veins.

The shower turned off, and Lizzie looked up from her little ball of light. James was still on the other side of the door, wet, naked, and probably warm.

A slow smile spread across her face.

What good was having power if you couldn't have a little fun with it?

Slipping out of bed, Lizzie crept to the door just as James finished tying a towel around his trim waist. It took all her self-control not to abandon her mission and slip inside to coerce him back into the shower.

Where they could both get wet and soapy.

There will be plenty of time for that.

James faced the mirror and started to run a comb through his messy hair.

Waving her hand, Lizzie mouthed, "*Titim.*" She grinned when James' towel dropped to the ground, revealing the rest of his gorgeous, tan skin.

"What the fuck?" he muttered, bending to pick it up.

Lizzie stepped away, covering her mouth and trying like hell to contain her fit of giggles. Once she'd managed to compose herself, she returned to the crack in the door to find James had re-covered himself with the towel. Lizzie repeated her joke, and it slipped once again from his waist, falling to the tiled floor in a messy heap.

James cursed again as it fell, and Lizzie had to step even further away to keep him from hearing her stifled laughter.

Sneaking back to the door, she spied James as he bent over and retrieved the towel a second time. Unable to resist toying with him some more, Lizzie gestured to the towel again, this time murmuring, "*Teacht chugam.*"

Come to me.

The towel slipped from his waist and flew out the door, right into her waiting arms.

James turned to where she stood, a knowing grin on his face.

Lizzie burst into laughter. Her sides hurt as she backed toward the bed, eyes watering from laughing so hard.

"Think that's funny, huh?" James asked calmly, leaning against the door frame with his arms crossed and a wide smile still in place.

"I really do," she said with a snort, which only made her laugh harder.

"You know, I may not be a Druid, but that doesn't mean I don't have magic of my own."

The way his hazel eyes narrowed on her face had Lizzie's mouth watering. "Oh yeah? Prove it," she teased.

"I think I just might have to."

She threw the towel at him and turned to make a run for it, but James caught her. He wrapped his arms around her waist, pulling her up against his still slightly damp body. Lizzie's laughter turned breathless when James' fingers dug into her ribs, tickling her mercilessly.

"Not fair!" she cried.

"You want to talk about fair? You stripped me naked three times, not even giving me a chance to return the favor."

He pressed a kiss to her neck, and Lizzie cocked her head to the side, unable to resist the feel of his lips against her skin.

"I didn't realize you needed help getting me naked," she joked.

"The least you could do is not use your unfair advantage on me."

"Where's the fun in that?"

She spun, and he released her. James continued

crossing the room after her, and Lizzie backed up until the backs of her legs hit the bed.

"You will pay for that," he said, leaning down so his mouth was only a breath away from hers.

"You promise?" she asked, lifting an eyebrow.

"I promise." James leaned down and brushed his lips against hers. Wrapping an arm around her, he laid her back against the mattress and climbed on top of her.

"I think I should remove your towel more often," she whispered against his mouth.

James pulled back just enough to look into her eyes. "Only if it means you're removing your clothes, too."

Lizzie grinned. "Deal."

"I love you, Lizzie."

"Love you, too, James."

Closing the distance between them, James took her mouth again, and Lizzie wrapped her arms around his neck, holding him close.

If amazing sex is what he considers payback, I'm going to have to screw with him more often.

CHAPTER 32

SKYE

Skye listened to the sounds of Lucas and Lizzie's bickering with a grin. Since returning to Chicago, the two had been at each other's throats about using their power. Lizzie was of the opinion that it only made sense that they enhance their lives with their new gifts, while Lucas was hesitant to touch his more than absolutely necessary.

Skye couldn't blame him; after everything they'd faced, and witnessing firsthand the power's ability to corrupt, wanting to tread carefully only made sense. Not that Skye had any lingering concerns that Lucas would ever misuse his power. He'd already proven otherwise.

"I should probably get in there before they whip out the rulers," Skye said with a grin as she turned to her computer screen.

Skye tried to fight back a laugh. No matter how many times they'd tried to tell her that she just had to talk facing the screen, Maggie couldn't seem to get the hang of it. Currently, Skye was staring up at her nostrils.

Maggie's mouth stretched across the screen as she leaned into the tiny webcam to ask, "Why would they need rulers, lass?"

"Never mind. I'll explain when I pick you and Giles up from the airport."

"Sounds good, dear. Ye take care now. Looking forward to this weekend."

"Us too. Bye, Maggie."

Hanging up, Skye sat back in her chair and stared up at the ceiling with a laugh. So much had changed in the last few weeks. After spending some time getting Maggie reacclimated to being home—and in the twenty-first century—Lucas received a call from his captain, begging him to come home. Although thrilled to see Lucas and James, Captain Daniels had been less than happy to return Lucy. He'd only let Lucas and Skye in when Lucas promised he'd bring the pup over for weekly visits.

The sound of James' booming laugh piqued her curiosity. Standing, Skye padded across the room, stumbling slightly when a familiar tingling started at the back of her neck.

She hadn't had any visions since the one in the Wasteland, and a sense of dread pooled in her stomach. Would it be death that waited for her? Skye barely made it back to her chair by the time the vision had her firmly in its grasp.

"Skye, baby, we've got to go. We're going to be late." Lucas poked his head around the door, whistling softly as he stared at her. "Wow."

"I look like a blimp." Skye sulked, staring at her reflection in the full-length mirror. Her dark hair was piled high on her head, soft curls falling down around her neck and shoulders.

"You look stunning."

Turning away from the mirror, her hands curled protectively around the swell of her stomach, Skye pouted. "Maids of honor should not look like they have a Thanksgiving turkey tucked beneath their dress."

Lucas laughed, stepping fully into the room. "No one is going to think you have a turkey in your dress," he promised, hand outstretched to rub her belly.

Skye rolled her eyes. "Pregnant women are supposed to glow, Lucas. I look like I could frighten small children." Skye turned back to the mirror, pinching her cheeks to add some color. "No amount of makeup in the world is going to make it look like I've gotten more than two hours of sleep a night the last month and a half."

Applying a dark red lipstick, Skye inspected herself in the mirror and scowled. "I don't even know why I'm bothering. Two seconds in, I'm going to start bawling like a baby. Pregnancy hormones are the worst."

Hiding his laugh behind his hand, Lucas moved to stand behind her and then placed both his hands on her shoulders. Kneading the knotted muscles, he said, "Nonsense, Giovanni. You are the most beautiful woman I've ever seen. And as soon as we get home from the wedding, I'm going to draw you a warm bath and then rub your feet for an hour."

Skye moaned in pleasure, her eyes fluttering closed at the thought. "I love you."

"I love you, too, baby. Now, let's go." He picked up her beaded bag from the bed and swatted her on the butt. "The best man can't be late to his sister's wedding."

"Especially since you're the one walking her down the aisle."

"Lizzie would never forgive me."

"And then James would have to defend her honor…it'd be a whole thing," Skye teased.

Lucas snorted. "Yeah right, ever since she got her power, Lizzie looks for excuses to light my ass up. There's no way she'd let Matthews fight her battle."

Skye wove her arm through his. "You're right. All the more reason to go. Can't have my sister-in-law murder my husband a month before her niece arrives."

"Niece? Yesterday, you were convinced it was a little boy."

Skye shrugged, pausing to let Lucas help her into her coat. "As long as our little one has blue eyes like their daddy, I'll be happy."

"No way, they're going to have golden eyes and dark curls like their mama."

Skye turned toward Lucas, her hand cupping his cheek. "How did I get so lucky to find a man like you?"

Lucas brushed his nose along the length of hers, pressing a soft kiss to her painted lips. "It was written in the stars, MacConnell. There was never any doubt we were going to end up right here, together."

~

SKYE BLINKED AWAY TEARS AS SHE STARED AT THE TOP OF her desk in awe.

"Giovanni, get your ass out here. Lizzie's cheating, and I need you to play interference before I throw her off the balcony."

"Hey!" Lizzie shouted.

Skye ignored them, her hands falling to her flat stomach as tears of wonder continued to fall. She was going to be a mother…a wife. *Holy shit.*

There was a quick knock on the door before it swung inward. "Hey, did you hear me?"

Wordlessly, Skye looked over to Lucas.

Rushing to her side, Lucas knelt beside her. "Baby? What's wrong? Why are you crying? Is everything okay with Nan?"

"Everything's fine," she assured him, brushing away her tears and grinning at him.

He gave her a skeptical look. "So, what's with the tears?"

Skye shook her head, not ready to share the secret that had been revealed to her, but Lucas was having none of it.

"Spill it, Giovanni."

"Not gonna happen, Detective," she said, standing.

Lucas stood and crossed his arms. "Wanna bet?" His lips were tilted in a sexy grin, and his blue eyes stared at her with a look that made her heart race.

Knowing they wouldn't make it out of the room anytime soon if he kept looking at her like that, Skye shrugged and said simply, "I had a vision."

Brows furrowing, he asked, "Who died?"

She shook her head. "No one. This time it was a life vision." She grinned at her little joke, even as her heart gave another flutter at what was waiting for them.

Lucas looked relieved, his smile growing. "So, the tears were relief, then?"

Skye nodded. "I Saw the future, and for once, I can't wait for it to come true."

Wrapping her in his arms, Lucas held her tight. "I don't need your gift to tell me what our future holds, Skye."

Tilting her head back to look up at him, she teased, "Me kicking your ass at cards?"

"You wish, Giovanni."

"Nah," Skye whispered, threading her fingers through his hair and pulling his face down toward hers. "I already have everything I wished for right here."

Thank you so much for reading! We hope you enjoyed Skye and Lucas's story! Please consider leaving an honest review! Reviews help us decide whether to continue writing in this world, as well as help other readers decide whether this is a literary journey they want to take!

Want to keep in touch? Sign up for Jessica Wayne's newsletter and download a free book! https://bit.ly/JWayneNLSubscribe

Sign up for Meg Anne's newsletter and receive updates on sales, as well as her new releases! MegAnneWrites.com/Newsletter

MEG'S ACKNOWLEDGMENTS

This is a bittersweet one for me. Writing with one of my best friends has been an incredible experience, and I am sad to see it come to an end, but so proud of how Skye and Lucas' journey concluded. Huge hugs and love to my co-author Jess, may you never run out of pickles and nacho cheese :P

To my husband, you are my biggest supporter and number one fan. I love you <3

Mom, I'll love you forever, I'll like you for always...

Melissa, Raye, Chanda, Heather - I'm pretty sure this book would still be only half-written if not for your words of encouragement and our daily sprints. Thanks for welcoming me into the fold :)

To my Chosen, thanks for sticking with me and for all your

thoughtful emails and messages. You guys are the reason I keep writing.

Fiona, Jessa, and Dominique, once again you've outdone yourselves. Your hard work makes our words shine. Couldn't do it without you.

I guess its time to start writing the next book…

Shazam
XOXO Meg

JESSICA'S ACKNOWLEDGMENTS

Wowza! I cannot believe it's already time to say goodbye to Lucas and Skye! Over the course of this series, I have learned so much, and getting to write with one of my best friends (who is also INCREDIBLY talented) has been a wonderful blessing!

Meg, our daily talks (whether we're chatting about the proper ingredients for a breakfast burrito, or plotting out what's going to happen next in our series) have become an incredibly important part of my day, and I couldn't imagine my life without you! I hope your life is always full of glitter!

To my amazing hubby, Nate. You are more than I could have ever asked for, the very person who gives me romantic inspiration daily. I could not survive without you and if ever there was a love story written in the stars, it's ours. I love you with all my heart!

To my kiddos who make my life such a crazy, wonderful adventure, follow your hearts and you can do anything. I love you!

To the Wayne-O's, thank you for being the best group of readers an author could ask for! You are the very reason I keep writing and your support is more important to me than I could even begin to explain!

Dominique (aka the best proofreader ever), your final touch on our manuscript really makes it shine, and I cannot thank you enough for all you do!

Jessa, thanks for all the edits, tips (even if some of them hurt lol), and for helping us put the finishing touches on our rough drafts!

To YOU the reader, without you none of this would be possible. Thank you for allowing me to live my dream!

'Slán go fóill'

(goodbye for now!).

Jessica

ABOUT MEG ANNE

Meg Anne has always had stories running on a loop in her head. They started off as daydreams about how the evil queen (aka Mom) had her slaving away doing chores; and more recently shifted into creating backgrounds about the people stuck beside her during rush hour. The stories have always been there; they were just waiting for her to tell them.

Like any true SoCal native, Meg enjoys staying inside curled up with a good book and her cat Henry... or maybe that's just her; sunburns hurt! You can convince Meg to buy just about anything if it's covered in glitter or rhinestones, or make her laugh by sharing your favorite bad joke. She also accepts bribes in the form of baked goods and Mexican food.

Meg loves to write about sassy heroines and the men that love them. She is best known for her fantasy romance series The Chosen.

Meg@MegAnneWrites.com

Want to know when I have a new release or get exclusive access to my works in progress?

Newsletter: MegAnneWrites.com/Newsletter
Website: MegAnneWrites.com
Readers Group:
facebook.com/groups/MegsChosen

ALSO BY MEG ANNE

The Chosen Series: The Complete Series

Mother Of Shadows

Reign Of Ash

Crown Of Embers

Queen Of Light

The Gypsy's Curse: The Complete Trilogy

Visions of Death

Visions of Vengeance

Visions of Triumph

The Keepers: The Complete Series

The Dreamer (A Keeper's Prequel)

The Keepers Legacy

The Keepers Retribution

The Keepers Vow

The Grimm Brotherhood: The Complete Trilogy

Reaper's Blood

Reaping Havoc

Reaper Reborn

Monster Ball Year 2: Contains Shade of Danger

(Undercover magic prequel)

ABOUT THE AUTHOR

Photo Credit Mandi Rose Photography

Jessica Wayne is the author of over fifteen fantasy and contemporary romance novels. The latter of which she writes as J.W. Ashley. During the day, she slays laundry and dishes as a homeschooling stay at home mom of three, and at night her worlds come to life on paper.

She runs on coffee and wine (as well as the occasional whiskey!) and if you ever catch her wearing matching socks, it's probably because she grabbed them in the dark.

She is a believer of dragons, unicorns, and the power of love, so each of her stories contain one of those elements (and in some cases all three).

Jessica lives in Texas with her husband, kids, their two German Shepherds who think they're both cats, and a fluffy orange cat named Leo who thinks he's a dog.

You can usually find her in her Facebook group, The Wayne-O's, or keep in touch by subscribing to her newsletter where she shares updates as well as shenanigans she finds herself in.

Stay Updated:

Newsletter: https://bit.ly/JWayneNLSubscribe
Website: https://www.jessicawayne.com
Readers Group: https://www.facebook.com/groups/JessicasWayneos

ALSO BY JESSICA WAYNE

THE TETHERED SAGA: THE COMPLETE SERIES

TETHERED SOULS

COLLATERAL DAMAGE

THE PROPHECY SERIES: THE COMPLETE SERIES

PHOENIX

FIGHTER

SORCERESS

THE GYPSY'S CURSE: THE COMPLETE TRILOGY

VISIONS OF DEATH

VISIONS OF VENGEANCE

VISIONS OF TRIUMPH

CAMBREXIAN REALM : THE COMPLETE SERIES

THE LAST WARD: FREE READ

WARRIOR OF MAGICK

GUARDIAN OF MAGICK

SHADES OF MAGICK

ROMANCE BY J.W. ASHLEY

THE CORRUPTED SERIES: THE COMPLETE TRILOGY

RESCUING NORAH

SHIELDING JEMMA

TARGETING CELESTE

STANDALONES

OLIVE YOU

THE LUMBERJACK EFFECT

LONG ROAD HOME

THE WHISKEY EFFECT: READ FOR FREE: HTTPS://BIT.LY/READWHISKEYEFFECTFREE

Made in the USA
Columbia, SC
30 July 2020

14184988R00181